OUT OF THE FIRE

JANE MORTIFEE

FG Publications, Vancouver, BC, Canada

OUT OF THE FIRE
© Jane Mortifee 2018

ISBN: 978-1-7751867-0-0

Cover Design by Diane Feught
Author Photo by Jane Green

FG Publications, Vancouver BC

www.janemortifee.com

OUT OF THE FIRE

CONTENTS

FOREWORD

MORNING	1
MAMA WIKAYA	3
BIRTH	4
IMBELEKO	8
WHITE MAN	11
MOON CYCLE	13
DEMON CHILD	18
VILLAGE LIFE	22
NTOMBI	24
HLWELO	28
CEREMONY	35
FIRE	40
GOGO AND NTOMBI	43
AFTERMATH	46
MANDLA	50
THE BEADED NECKLACE	54
HLWELO	60
NTOMBI	62
DOYENNE	70
NOMBULANI	75
WEDDING	79
TIME PASSING	91
INTO THE VELD	102
WANDISWE	106
COMPLETION	107
HLWELO'S JOURNEY	117
JOURNEYING	126
HEALING	132
THE VILLAGE	138
RETURN	146
RAIN	151

CHARACTER GUIDE	153
GLOSSARY	155
ACKNOWLEDGEMENTS	158
ABOUT THE AUTHOR	159

DEDICATION

To all my teachers...
those who have caused damage,
those who have facilitated healing,
and those I have yet to meet.

FOREWORD

I was born in South Africa and, although I was very young when we immigrated to Canada, the roots of the land of my early experience have resurfaced in these pages. It is a mystery to me that this book emerged at all as I never set out to write a novel, but rather took a creative writing course with Paul Belserene in UBC's Continuing Studies program, with the intention of writing songs for my next album. This book is the result of a prompt he gave, so to him I am deeply grateful... I think... as writing it was the hardest thing I have ever done. I have yet to write any songs.

Ntombi, the main character, insisted her way into my pen and would not leave me alone, eventually convincing me that she had chosen me to tell her story. I have used many Zulu words and names throughout the book, and even though my closest connection to a native culture in my youth was to the Zulus, the depiction of ceremonies and traditions is a combination of my exposure to indigenous cultures around the world and the recesses of my imagination. My apologies if anything described herein comes too close to the actual practices of any tribe and is perceived as incorrect or inappropriate. In writing this book it has been my sincere desire to honour the Great Wisdom and Mystery of all cultures and their profound connection to the Divine Universal Spirit.

MORNING

The Chief listened to the deep even breaths of his wife, Mama Wikaya. He smelled her warm skin and reached out his hand to touch her. It was not yet time to stir if she was still held in the depths of stillness. He slipped back into sleep, his eyes twitching as the dreamtime entered and took him. His mind dipped into the shadows and descended into the underworld. As he journeyed deeper his stomach tightened, sweat and heat rose on his skin. As his hands shot forward reaching for something, he awoke. He smelled burning wood and his flesh tingled as the memory of the dream lingered, just beyond his reach. He peered out of the hut and saw Mama Wikaya stoking the smouldering embers from the previous night's fire, adding small twigs and breathing life and flame into the wood. She was stirring the contents of the pot that was suspended above the fire. Whatever it was that had frightened him vanished back into the dreamtime. Mama Wikaya was safe, the village was safe, but even so the unease in his chest persisted.

The Chief roused himself and stepped out of the hut. He stood tall. His forehead was broad, his lips thick and full, his cheekbones high and distinct, his skin black as a raven. He looked out from his vantage point at the apex of the village. The animals were in their hold, eyes half-closed, breathing the slow breath of sleep. The children were still lost in their innocent dreams. The adults were beginning the climb up from the oblivion of night to the chores of the day. As the dark surrendered to the insistence of the light, the animals began to snort and shift, eyelids of beast and human alike fluttering to wakefulness. Throughout the village the soft pink light of a new day seeped its way into shapes and forms. Babies cried for their mothers' breast, young girls carried clay pots to the river, fragrant steam rose from the pots of *mealie meal* bubbling over crackling fires.

He was a well-respected Chief who ruled with a gentle but firm hand. His was a large village, a peaceful one. He governed over many homesteads and he smiled as he looked out over the vast land and the pleasing symmetry that met his eye. The young boys were beginning to herd the cattle and goats from the *isibaya* to the veld. The crops rustled in the fields at the bottom of the slope just outside the perimeter of the *muzi*. He was enjoying watching the life of his village when Mama Wikaya approached him carrying a bowl of water. She offered it to him with her head bowed, a gentle smile on her lips.

"*Inkosi*, your meal is ready," she said.

The Chief lifted the bowl to his lips and taking a sip of water, swirled it around his mouth and, according to custom, turned away from his wife and spat it onto the ground. He then dipped his hands in the water and rinsed them. He looked at her, admiring her stout body. Her hair was woven through with grasses and red threads crowning her head in a magnificent wide headdress. On the nights he slept with her he marveled at her ability to sleep with her neck cradled in the carved wooden pillow crafted to accommodate that large headdress. Once he had even tried to sleep on it, but quickly abandoned it, shaking his head at yet another of the many differences between men and women that he would never comprehend. He looked now at the shape of her broad hips under her skirt. He reached out his hand and touched the soft strips of leather sewn together. He looked at the shape of her large breasts where the colourful beads fell between them onto the thin impala skin pulled up across her one shoulder and tucked under the other arm. Of his three wives, she was his first and he loved her the best. He turned to see his two other wives fussing together to make sure all was as it should be for him. He looked to the sky and thanked the Ancestors for his great good fortune and with a sigh tried to let go of the worry with which the dream had left him.

MAMA WIKAYA

Mama Wikaya balanced the empty clay pot atop her head and ambled down to the river. Other women along the way nodded their heads in respect as they passed. Mama Wikaya was well-liked by the women of the village. She had an even, friendly way of greeting them all. Even though, as the First Wife of the Chief, she did not need to fetch her own water, she preferred to do it. It was one of the ways she retained her connection to these women, a sisterhood she never wanted to lose by virtue of her position.

She slipped the clay pot from her head and filled it with the sweet water, then made her way to the brewery hut. She set the pot on the hard earth floor. She still enjoyed making beer for her husband and was not yet ready to hand over this duty to one of the other wives. From the large containers that lay almost completely buried in the floor of the hut, she took handfuls of coarse sorghum and maize, mixed them into fresh water, then set the pot aside. The day before she had made the same mixture. She stoked the fire, then placed yesterday's pot over the flames and stirred until it began to bubble. Yeasty fragrance rose and circled the hut. She sat and waited until she detected the subtle change in sound and smell, then added more dry sorghum to the mash, stirred it and set it aside to cool.

She took a long thin cone-shaped basket down from a hook on the wall. She held the pointed end over a hollowed-out gourd and from yet another pot poured the three-day-old fermented liquid into the wide opening at the top. She squeezed the basket, wringing it with her strong hands until all the cloudy liquid seeped through the woven reeds, spilling over her fingers and into the waiting calabash. She took the basket outside, dumped out the leftover bits of mash and repeated the process until the last drop of liquid had drained into the gourd. Today's beer was now ready for the Chief.

BIRTH

Lindiwe swept in front of her hut, struggling with the rolling contractions in her belly. Having been through this three times before, she knew the baby was getting ready. It wouldn't be long now. Lwazi, her youngest child, ran circles around her, laughing and trying to catch the ends of the reed broom in his little hands with each sweep. Lindiwe watched her husband, Dinzane, tall and handsome, as he emerged from his hut, spear in hand. He came to her. She placed her hand over his as he gently caressed her bulging belly. She smiled as he bent down and whispered to the unborn child, "I will see you soon, little man, maybe even today if the Gods will it so." He stroked Lwazi's cheek. "You be sure to be a good boy for *umama* while I am gone," he said and turned to go off for the day's hunt.

Lindiwe watched as he joined the other men, their greetings hearty and friendly. Another contraction spread across her belly as she saw the men leaving through the village gate. With a gush, the membranes broke and the birth water streamed down her thighs and knees and splashed onto the dirt, pooling around the outline of her feet before disappearing into the earth. She winced and let out a moan. She went into her hut and dried herself as best she could with a mud-cloth wrap. She took Lwazi by his hand, called for her elder son, Sandiwe, and together they waddled over to where the grandmothers sat weaving long river reeds into strong baskets.

"The new baby is coming," she said.

Lwazi ran to his grandmother, "Gogo!" he beamed as he took her outstretched hand. He nestled himself next to her knees breathing in the musty smell of her mud-cloth wrap. He took the river reeds she held out to him and furrowed his brow as he tried to replicate the crossing of one reed over another.

Lindiwe kissed Lwazi and then Sandiwe. She steadied herself as her belly contracted again. She nodded to her mother and the other grandmothers and left to look for the midwives of the village.

"We have been waiting for you," Themba said. "I said to Msama last night that it would be in the morning of tomorrow when this new being will decide to make its appearance, and here you are, just as I predicted."

Msama laughed and said, "Yes, it is so, it is what she said to me last night."

The two women went to either side of Lindiwe and, offering their hands, walked with her to the birthing hut at the outskirts of the village. With each step Lindiwe allowed the women to support more of her weight. She was in pain and more than ready to have this baby leave her body and enter into the world of her family and her village. She felt relief in the dim light as she entered the hut. With each child, she had welcomed leaving the bright light of the day and going into the dark and quiet to breathe and sweat her way through the birthing process.

The pains came and went with less and less time between each wave. Lindiwe cried out as they intensified. Finally Themba gave the signal and Lindiwe held her breath, closed her eyes and pushed, keeping the sound of her efforts inside her. She gasped for breath, took another deep inhale and pushed again.

"That is good," Themba said, "you're doing fine."

Lindiwe stopped pushing, her breath short and shallow. After a few minutes of rest her body resumed its urge to push and she sucked in a full breath and pushed again. The baby's head appeared, splitting Lindiwe's skin with its imminent arrival. Blood leaked onto the mat.

"Keep going," Themba said, "the baby is almost here, keep going."

Lindiwe pushed and gasped again and again, sweat thick on her face, until the baby shot forth into Themba's waiting hands. Themba took the small reed from beside her on the mat and sucked from the baby's nostrils, spitting bits of birth onto the floor. She wiped the blood from the little body. "You have a beautiful baby girl," she said. She wrapped the child in a mud-cloth and passed her to Lindiwe. All was quiet in the hut as the midwives watched the first few moments of mother and child together, waiting to see if this baby was strong. They remembered the deep sadness they had all felt when Lindiwe's last little girl had died only moments after her birth.

"Thank you, Themba," Lindiwe smiled weakly, "I wanted a little girl. Ntombi."

Lindiwe looked at her newborn, counted her fingers, unwrapped the cloth and counted her toes. She sent up a heartfelt prayer to the Ancestors asking that this one be allowed to live and grow strong and healthy. The baby's mouth began to move, the lips pursing forward. Lindiwe positioned the baby at her breast and brushed her nipple against the baby's cheek. The baby turned its head and as the tip of the nipple made contact with the baby's lips, milky liquid oozed from the tiny opening. The baby's mouth opened wide, engulfed the large hard nipple and began to suck. Lindiwe smiled at the force with which the baby sucked and swallowed. She sighed with relief. As the milk was pulled from deep within her breast Lindiwe's belly contracted again and, with a sharp shudder from deep within her womb, the afterbirth spilled out onto the mat.

Themba gathered it into a bowl. Then she gently cleaned Lindiwe's woman place with fresh water and soothed her torn flesh with a mixture of crushed aloe and honey.

Msama began cleaning the hut, taking the soiled mat and cloths away and replacing them with fresh ones. When the space had been thoroughly cleaned she went to find Dinzane and tell him he could now enter and greet his new child.

Dinzane entered the hut. He saw the baby sucking at Lindiwe's full breast. It was a soothing sound that spread like warm sun throughout his limbs. He watched as Lindiwe opened the wrap that enfolded the child. A girl. Dinzane felt a wave of disappointment cross his heart. Even though he knew it was what Lindiwe had so desparately desired, he wanted more male hands to help provide for his increasing family. He went to Lindiwe's side. He looked into the eyes of the child and a curious sensation formed in his chest. It was unfamiliar, unsettling. He reached out his hands to take the child. He felt big and clumsy as he held the fragility of her newness. His rough hands barely registered the downy softness of her skin. He lifted her up and pressed her against his heart, the warmth and softness of her entering his chest. His body tingled and he held very still.

Lindiwe was unsure. She could not read Dinzane's face.

"I'm sorry," she said, "I know you were hoping for another boy. Perhaps the next child will fulfill your wishes."

Dinzane shook his head. "You have done well, Lindiwe." He paused then added, "I feel the Ancestors inside this small body."

He gently returned the child to Lindiwe, kissed her cn the forehead and left the hut. He walked out of the village, up to the top of a rocky cliff and sat looking over the land and the quiet village. The dull ache in his chest was neither happy nor sad, and was also both at the same time. A shiver passed through him. Dinzane didn't like things to be complicated. He preferred the predictability of his life and somehow he sensed this was going to change.

In the hut, Lindiwe gathered up the child and, with the help of Themba and Msama, took the bowl of afterbirth to the isibaya. She dug a hole under the Buffalo Thorn tree. As she poured the contents of the bowl into the waiting earth, she asked the Ancestors to watch over her little girl, her little Ntombi, to keep her safe from harm. She covered the bloody mass with dirt and hid the freshly disturbed ground from view with some leaves from the tree so no bad spirits would find the place and interfere with Ntombi's life.

Gogo was waiting with Lwazi and Sandiwe when Lindiwe returned to her hut. She put her arms around her daughter. "I have already heard you have a baby girl," she said, "I hope you are as happy as I was when you were born. I have been blessed with having you for my daughter and now I am blessed with a beautiful granddaughter. Now, we must prepare for the *Imbeleko*."

IMBELEKO

Nyongo felt the gentle touch as Jabulile traced her fingers lightly over the tough black skin of his back. His breath deepened and he rolled towards her encircling her with his arms, smiling at the familiar scent of her willingness. Nyongo and Jabulile had grown up together, had always loved each other, first with the innocence of children, then with the deep connection of mature love. To him, she was like a flower with an immense beauty and a smell that would open his heart and arouse his body.

"Today is the Imbeleko to introduce Lindiwe and Dinzane's baby to the Ancestors," Jabulile sighed. Too much time had passed, and still she had not borne him a child. "I'm sorry my body does not receive your children," she said. "I do not know what is wrong with me."

Nyongo was silent. He, too, was disappointed. He loved Jabulile, but the men of the village would not see him as a man until he had sired a child. He had wondered if he should ask for the return of the nine cows from her father, the lobola he had paid for her. But that would bring shame to her and her family and he did not want that. Perhaps he should just take another wife…after all, it was time for him to do so. But he had been waiting, hoping for a child with Jabulile before taking to the mat with another woman.

"We will see what the Ancestors have decided for our future. I will be home early to come to the Imbeleko with you and celebrate with the village. Perhaps one day soon we will have the village attend the presentation of our child to the Ancestors."

After their breakfast, Nyongo kissed his woman on the lips and set off. He crossed through the village with a nod and words of congratulations to Dinzane as he passed by him along his customary route. At his work area on the slope above the village, he set about making a small, hot fire. Here he placed the rocks he had previously selected for the good quality of iron that lay within them. He took comfort in his familiar routine. As the fire smelted the iron from the ore, he watched the molten liquid trickle along the thin groove dug into the earth and down the incline into the mould carved into the hard ground. Waiting for the metal to cool, Nyongo squatted by the dying fire and gazed out over the expanse of land beyond the village.

"One day," he thought, "I will teach a son how to read the earth so he, too, can become a master spearmaker. I pray the Ancestors will hear my request."

After he had fashioned the new spearhead, Nyongo returned to his hut. Jabulile was ready, dressed in her best wrap, feet freshly washed. He picked up the gourd of beer to present to the new parents and together they set off to the celebration. When they arrived many villagers were already there, some helping with the fire, some crowding around the new baby with words of welcome and congratulations. Nyongo presented the beer to Dinzane with the customary greeting of clasping right hands and touching foreheads. He then placed the gourd with the other offerings. He and Jabulile gathered with the others as Nomalanga, Lindiwe's mother, grandmother to Lwazi and Sandiwe, came forward with the new child in her arms. The crowd grew quiet.

"As the family elder I am here today to present this child to the Ancestors and ask for their protection."

While she spoke, Dinzane held his sharpened knife in one hand and a goat's head in his other, his legs pressed together to hold the squirming animal steady.

As Nomalanga raised the child above her head she called out the chosen names, "Our beloved Ancestors, we present to you, Bisisiwe… this baby is blessed, Thabisile…this baby has brought joy…Lungile… this person is good…"

As she spoke and explained the meanings of each name, Dinzane lifted the head of the goat and, with a quick and clean stroke, sliced through its neck.

"Protect and guide this new life…" the blood spilled freely into a hollowed out calabash.

"Keep watch over her so she may grow strong and have many children of her own…"

Dinzane let go of the goat head which hung limp, the eyes clear but unseeing. He brought the calabash to Nomalanga who dipped her finger in the warm liquid and placed a drop on the baby's forehead, officially sealing the name of Bisisiwe Thabisile Lungile. Ululations from the women grew loud and joyous. The celebrations began.

Nyongo looked at Jabulile with a sad smile and left to help the men. Jabulile's ululations ceased as she watched him go. She joined the women and helped them build the fire for the celebratory meal. The men expertly slit the belly of the goat, its entrails falling on the ground. They retrieved the gall bladder so it could dry and hang in Lindiwe's hut. They made sure the animal's skin was cleaned of all the bits of clinging meat and then cut a small piece the length of the pelt. They gave it to Nomalanga to wind into a little bracelet for the child. Wearing this assured the Ancestors they had been honoured. They hung the skin outside of Lindiwe's hut to dry. It was to be the baby's first blanket. They carved the meat into chunks, collected the bones and took all of it to the women at the fire.

Lindiwe hugged Nomalanga. "Thank you, mother, you are now Gogo yet again. My daughter is well-named but to me she will always be my little girl, my Ntombi."

Nomalanga smiled. "I, too, will always think of her as Ntombi, and I very much like being Gogo once again. It sits well with me." And with those words she tied the bracelet of goatskin around Ntombi's little wrist to seal the protection of the Ancestors.

WHITE MAN

When Nyongo and Jabulile arose the next morning, both felt subdued. After the morning meal, Nyongo left to continue making his spears. Jabulile went up the river to gather berries. When she had walked a long way she found them, abundant, bright red and plump against the low stalks. Carefully, she pulled the ripe berries from their stems and placed them in a hollowed gourd. She smelled the river, fresh and inviting. She tasted the berries, their sweet juices bursting in her mouth.

She heard an unfamiliar sound. She looked up to see a white man on horseback approaching the riverbed. He brought his horse to a stop beside her. Jabulile had never seen a man like this before. She had heard stories that they existed but had not believed them to be true. His skin was the colour of ostrich eggs and his eyes the colour of new shoots that appear after the first rains. She was fascinated. He opened his mouth and strange sounds came out. Jabulile was puzzled. He took a small sack off his saddle, pointed to the river then threw the sack at her feet. She put down the half-filled gourd of berries, slowly stepped forward, took the container and went and filled it in the river. The white man got off his horse and waited for her to bring him the water. He drank his fill and gestured for her to do it again. As she handed him the refilled sack he grabbed her by the wrist. His foot kicked over the gourd scattering the berries over the rocks and sand.

Jabulile tried to pull away, shoots of fear racing through her limbs, but his grasp was strong. She tried to scream but her throat froze, her mouth gaping open and closed like a dying fish. She pulled and struggled and his fist found her cheek. She reeled, the sky swirling above her. Another blow, this time on her mouth, the blood falling freely down her chin and neck.

After the white man had finished, he mounted his horse and rode away. Jabulile lay on the ground. Semen mixed with blood darkened the earth as it left her body. She picked herself up from the disturbed ground and waded into the river. She cupped the water into her hands and, as gently as she could, tried to wash herself clean of what had been left behind. Her hands trembled. Jabulile had only ever known Nyongo. Her body had always opened with the juices of her love for him with no pain, except perhaps for a little on their first love mat. Now her insides felt raw and enflamed. She tried to cool the burning with the help of the gentle river but after only momentary relief, the pain would resume. Jabulile walked out of the river, gathered the upset berries, placed them back in the gourd and returned to the village. She quietly entered the hut without having been noticed.

When Nyongo returned home he found Jabulile huddled in the corner of the hut, her knees held close to her chest. Even in the dim light he could see the distortion of her face. He held her carefully as she recounted what had happened at the river. Together they wept as Nyongo held his rage inside his body, knowing it was useless to think of avenging his wife. He would never find this white man. He could never reclaim her honour for her. He could never undo what had been done.

Moon Cycle

Jabulile did not return to her exuberant self, but rather went through her days with a dull feeling in her heart. Nyongo was patient and tender with her until she was ready to receive his body inside hers again. They were both grateful to share themselves with each other once more but the wild abandon they used to experience in their lovemaking was gone, replaced now by caution and sadness.

She waited for her moon cycle but the blood did not come. Her body shivered cold on the inside. Perhaps tomorrow the blood would begin. But tomorrow brought no blood. Neither did the next day, nor the next.

"Nyongo, I am afraid," she said, her voice quiet. "We have waited so long for a child, and yet…" Nyongo looked at his beautiful wife, at the worry etched around her soft eyes. He himself had been aware of the passing days and that she had not yet removed herself from his sleeping mat as she did every month at the fruition of her moon cycle.

"All may still be well," he said trying to believe that it might be so. He went to her side and placed his broad hand on her belly feeling the rise and fall of her breath, feeling the warmth of her body enter his hand. "It may be our happiness growing inside you. The Ancestors may have answered our prayers."

Jabulile smiled. "You are a kind man," she said as she folded herself into him, hoping to absorb some of this strength and optimism.

The months passed and her belly grew. Jabulilie tried to imagine the seed sprouting inside her was from her beloved Nyongo, but deep inside her body she feared what was growing there. One morning, as Jabulile was stirring the mealie meal, she felt movement deep within her belly. In spite of her fears, she grinned at the miracle of another life announcing itself. Then another sensation… a foot perhaps or was it a fist? She imagined the perfectly formed body swimming inside her.

"Nyongo," she called, "come quickly." Nyongo emerged from the hut.

"Here, give me your hand." She grasped his outstretched hand and quickly pulled him closer placing his hand on her roundness. Nothing.

She looked at Nyongo.

"Wait, wait…" Her belly jumped. "There…did you feel that?" Her eyes were dancing.

"Yes," he said, "does it hurt?"

"No," she laughed.

Hearing the ease in her voice, Nyongo laughed, too, and hugged her close as he sent up another silent prayer to the Ancestors.

At last the hour came when the internal waters burst and the birthing pains began.

Nyongo was sent away while Themba and Msama came to walk Jabulile to the birthing hut.

The hours stretched by, the contractions coming in quick succession and then tapering off. It was a long process, too long, and the women began to fear that the baby would never come. Msama crushed herbs and mixed them with clay from the riverbank and smeared the poultice across Jabulile's taut belly. Themba mixed other herbs with goat milk and encouraged Jabulile to drink. They sang, they chanted. It seemed as if nothing would encourage this stubborn baby to come out and greet the world.

Two days passed. Jabulile was exhausted. At the dawn of the third day, from deep within her, a scream arose and with it her baby was forced into the open air. Themba caught the wrinkled, mottled mass as it shot its way into the world and quickly sucked through a hollow reed to clear its nostrils.

As they wiped the baby's body clean, the women who had been so vocal with their songs of encouragement lapsed into silence. His skin was a strange pale shade they had never seen before. Themba looked at Jabulile as she brought the child up to place it in her arms. "You have a son," she said tentatively.

Jabulile saw the colour of the baby and a cry escaped from her lips. She kissed his forehead, holding her lips against his skin for as long as she could, until her arms trembled with exhaustion and she lost the strength to hold him. Themba's eyes grew big as she saw too much blood still running from Jabulile's body.

"Msama, hurry, take care of the baby, then hold Jabulile still." Msama took the child, quickly cut the umbilical cord, and laid him on the mat. She went and knelt by Jabulile's head.

Themba turned to Jabulile and said, "This will be painful but we must act quickly. Breathe deeply now."

Themba reached her hand into the vacant womb and, while massaging the outside of the belly, grasped the fibrous sac and pulled it out as gently as she could. Jabulile's body tried to jolt upright but was held in place by Msama's hands pressing down on her shoulders. She moaned, tears of pain streaming down her cheeks. The baby whimpered. The afterbirth spilled out but the blood did not stop. Again Themba put her hand inside Jabulile and with her other hand massaged the top of her belly hoping to stem the flow of blood but it continued… horrible, thick, dark red pools surrounding Jabulile's woman place and thighs.

"Msama, bring the women to help clean up this blood." She looked at Jabulile and looking away quietly said, "and I think we must bring Nyongo."

Nyongo had been sharpening his spearheads. He was determined to be calm and productive while Jabulile engaged in that unknowable woman's mystery of childbirth. How many times had he rested his hand upon her twitching belly, the unborn life feeling its way around its tiny world? How many times had he pushed away dark thoughts of the possible moment that its life took form?

The blade sliced into his finger, dark red blood sprang from the wound. Nyongo cursed himself for his inability to stay focused. He laid down the spear. It was useless to pretend he could concentrate. He returned to the hut, cut a long thin strip of animal hide and walked out into the savannah. He found an aloe plant and, carefully skinning the tough, sharp-toothed outer layer, removed a section of yellow slimy sap, placed it on the cut and bound the severed edges tight with the strip of goat hide. He sliced another piece of aloe and ate it, hoping to quiet the unrest in his stomach.

He had waited too long. Three days was too long for a baby to be born, even he knew that. He looked to the sky and prayed to the Ancestors to ask the Gods directly, "Please keep Jabulile safe."

"Nyongo!"

He heard his name called. A rush of fear ran through him. Msama came running to him.

"You have a son, but it is not good with Jabulile. You must come." Nyongo ran to the hut.

Themba was at the entrance. "You cannot enter yet, Nyongo, it is not clean." "I don't care," cried Nyongo, "let me go to her."

"You cannot! It is not yet clean! You cannot!"

Nyongo smacked his hands against his head, teeth clenched, breath short and laboured. Women bearing pots of water on their heads entered and left with armloads of bloodied cloth, their eyes lowered, skirting wide around him. He didn't look into their eyes. He was stunned by the amount of blood they carried.

Themba placed thick folds of cloth between Jabulile's legs and placed a skin over her naked body. At last she appeared at the entrance to the hut. "You may come in now," she said, and stepping aside let Nyongo through the opening.

The hut was dim and quiet. Jabulile looked at Nyongo and whispered, "I'm sorry."

All Nyongo could see were the hollow eyes of his beloved. He heard her take a small breath and let it go, and he heard no more. Nyongo sank to his knees and hung his head. He crawled across the floor to the side of his dead love. Her face was sad and worn, there was no trace left of the joy they had once shared. He heard a small sound, and there on the mat lay this strange creature, the pale skin confirming his worst fears. Yes, it was a son, but Nyongo's heart could not rejoice. How was he to care for this horrific reminder of the violation and death of his wife? An acrid smell rose from his skin. His belly began to churn.

Helpless in a raging tide of torment, he cursed the white man for raping his beautiful Jabulile. He cursed this baby for killing her. He cursed the Ancestors for allowing any of this to happen. Spasms of rage contracted his chest. He looked at the ghostly boy, tormented with visions of hurling the small, discoloured body off the top of the rock cliffs, avenging his wife's death, one life for another.

He turned to the midwives but the hut was empty. He was alone. A wail of grief erupted, the sound penetrating the walls of the dim hut. Nyongo fell in defeat onto Jabulile's body. How was he to go on without his beautiful woman? How was he to care for this boy when he could not stand to look at him?

"Help me, Jabulile, help me, I don't think that I can do this," he wept.

He ran his hand over Jabulile's damp head, a tangle of hair coming away in his hand. His heart twisted with despair. When his breathing eventually slowed and his tears subsided he reached out his trembling hands and, keeping Jabulile's hair in his grasp, picked up the whimpering child. It was the only part left of her that he could still hold. He looked once again into her quiet face and vowed on her still-warm body that he would do everything within his power to care for this boy, to nurture him, and help him find his way in a life that would be constantly challenged by the otherness of his skin. And he vowed to fight the demons inside himself that would want to punish him for killing her.

DEMON CHILD

News spread quickly throughout the village that a demon child had been born to Nyongo and that it had already killed Jabulile. A mist of fear seeped into the village.

The Chief knew something was wrong. He felt a jolt move up through the ground, his feet, his spine, and land in his heart. He called for Mama Wikaya.

"What is it?" he said. "What has happened?"

Mama Wikaya lifted her gaze and looked straight into his eyes.

"Jabulile is dead. She birthed a demon child the colour of the moon who killed her." A chill rippled through her body as she spoke.

The Chief closed his eyes and took a breath. After a pause he said, "Fill my water skin and bring me a pouch of *biltong*. I will go to the Sangoma and hear what the bones have to say."

Mama Wikaya brought the provisions to the Chief. "*Hambagahle*, go well my husband," she said.

"*Hlalagahle*," he replied.

The Chief walked through the village, his eyes sharp, his stride strong and quick. He made his way out through the savannah, leaving the day behind as he walked up over the hills to the hut of the Sangoma. He paused at the foot of a rocky incline. Large boulders, holding the heat of the day, stood sentinel. He waited, eyes intent on the turn in the path ahead. He waited, feeling the warmth from the rocks on his skin, the firmness of the ground below his feet. Shoshoni, the Sangoma, appeared. The Chief lowered his gaze and, extending his hand, offered the parcel of dried meat.

"I have come to ask for your help. I must know if an evil spirit has entered my village."

"Come," Shoshani said, "We will call the Ancestors."

Shoshani led the Chief past the bend in the path to a clearing in front of a mud hut.

"Sit here," he said, pointing to a large flat stone close to a small fire, then disappeared into the hut. He re-emerged and laid out an impala skin in front of the Chief. On it he placed a curved piece of calabash filled with white heather. He took a small stick from the fire and ignited the dried plant. Tendrils of smoke snaked into the air, its fragrance pungent and sweet. Shoshani picked up the gourd and, cupping his hand, waved the smoke around the head and shoulders of the Chief, then around his own body. His lips moved in silent supplication. He placed the gourd to the side. He untied a small sack that hung from the cloth at his waist, shook it, blew into it three times, had the Chief do the same, then tossed its contents onto the impala skin. Small pieces of bone, teeth and shell tumbled into place. He breathed deeply, his eyes rolled up disappearing under their lids, only the whites left showing. His body shook and then was still. His pupils reappeared. He surveyed the placement of the bones.

"It is not an evil spirit that has entered your village. It is the embodiment of a great wrong done to one of your women. She was in the path of a ghost man who was driven by hate and fear. It cost her her life. There is a child who carries these seeds of anger. They colour his skin and will colour his life. Be careful with him. He will need guidance and help."

The Chief sat for a long time feeling a great sadness.

"Thank you," he said, looking into the eyes of the Sangoma.

He bowed his head until it touched the earth. Shoshani bowed his head touching the earth. The men stood.

The Chief said, "Hlalagahle, stay in peace."

"Hambagahle," Shoshani said, "go in peace."

The Chief walked back to his village under the darkened sky. He went to Mama Wikaya's hut.

"The child is not a demon. You must go to Nyongo and help him. Show him how to feed and tend to his son. This is how we can honour Jabulile's memory and prevent evil from growing in our village."

Nyongo was awkward as he cared for the boy as best he could. He felt the stares from the villagers and the isolation. No one from the village would come near. He kept the umbilical cord clean and offered strips of soft leather soaked in goat's milk to the suckling newborn as Mama Wikaya had instructed him. It took eight days for the stump extending from the baby's body to fall. As was tradition, Nyongo went to bury it in the ground of the isibaya, so no matter where the boy might travel, this village would always be his home.

He prayed to the Ancestors as he dug into the orange earth. His fingers sifted through the coarse dirt, digging deeper as if to bury the losses of the past and the fears for the future along with the shriveled piece of skin. He prayed for the boy's safety, for a place for him in the community. He also prayed for himself, for the strength to be a loving and wise father when everything in him wanted to run from this lonely responsibility. He covered the umbilical cord with soil, cut a branch from the Buffalo Thorn tree and placed it over the disturbed earth asking the Ancestor's spirits within the branch to watch over this boy, to stay close by him. He named him Hlwelo Sinhawukele… Hlwelo, the one who conquers in hopeless situations, Sihawukele…have mercy on us.

Nyongo sat for a long time. He looked at the fresh mound of earth covered by the branch. Hate had been rising in his chest since the day of Jabulile's violation. He knew it was wrong to hate but it snaked its way up his spine and gripped his heart at times when he was too tired and too sad to fight it. He prayed that with his new name the boy would be able to find his way. He remembered the Imbeleko for Ntombi. There would be no such celebration for Hlwelo.

Nyongo returned to the hut and the sleeping child. He picked up a piece of stinkwood and went down to the riverbed and began carving. His sharp blade cut into the dark flesh of the wood. His eyes were set with purpose. He turned the wood this way and that, scraping, shaping, calling forth a shape in which to hold his grief. He wept onto the wood. Spittle fell from his mouth. His chest burned. His arms fell to his sides, one hand holding the blade, the other gripping the half-made box. His head fell back, a gutteral sound wrenching up from his belly, exploding into the hot air. Wave after wave of piercing cries. He lifted the wood to his cheek and stroked his skin with its unfinished surface. He took the blade and sliced into his flesh, the blood seeping into the grain undulating through the wood.

The sound within him spent, he sank to his haunches and began again to work the wood. Every twist of the blade deepened the groove, widening the space in which to hold his love. Nyongo went to the stream and, scooping up fine gravel, rubbed it around the inside of the box, over and over until his fingers bled and the wood became smooth. He did the same with the snug-fitting lid. He made sure it was difficult to open.

He returned to his hut and took the leather pouch from the hook on the wall. He carefully removed the wiry strands of curls he had taken from Jabulile's still body and, prying open the box, placed them inside, re-securing the lid. There, contained inside the box, was his own blood and his love's hair.

He buried the box inside the isibaya under the Buffalo Thorn tree, next to the umbilical cord of the boy, asking the Ancestors to watch over this love he had shared with his dead wife and to keep her safe until he could join her.

VILLAGE LIFE

As time passed, the village settled into a rhythm of daily life that tolerated the presence of Hlwelo, mostly out of respect for Nyongo and for the suffering he had endured through the loss of his wife and the burden of such a son. Nyongo abandoned the hut he had shared with Jabulile, unable to be in the presence of memories that filled the clay walls. Nyongo had no heart to take another wife. He and his son lived together in a hut at the edge of the village.

Over the years Hlwelo grew tall and lean but he remained aloof from the other children, his eyes narrowing with distrust whenever he saw a group of them together. He understood his difference was not welcomed and he kept his distance.

One day as he walked too close to the children of the village playing together by the fire pit, Mwele, the largest of the group looked up and saw him. He laughed out loud, a contemptible sound.

"What's wrong with you, anyway?"

The children who had been laughing and jostling against each other stopped and stared at Hlwelo. Mwele picked up ash from the fire-pit, rubbed it over his body mirroring the appearance of Hlwelo's discoloured skin. He danced around Hlwelo in a grotesque mockery, laughing and jeering. Some of the others joined in.

Hlwelo's eyes grew dark, his fists clenched. His body coiled, ready to spring.

Ntombi rushed forward pushing Mwele hard.

"Stop it," she shouted. Ntombi's face was hot. Her flashing eyes glared at Mwele. "What's wrong with you?" she spat. And with tears restrained behind her eyes, she turned back to Hlwelo.

Hlwelo was breathing hard, his mind a jumble. He was relieved he didn't have to fight the massive Mwele, angry that his skin had once again singled him out, humiliated that a girl had saved him and puzzled by the clutching around his heart when he looked at Ntombi. He wanted to thank her for not joining in the laughter with the others but he was afraid that it might come out wrong and she would end up laughing at him after all.

Hlwelo looked at her, at Mwele, then at the others who were now standing silent. He turned his back and walked away, his teeth grinding and his jaw rigid.

NTOMBI

L indiwe was tired and could tell that her good-natured new baby girl would soon slip into her nap.

"Ntombi, little Bonisiwe will soon be sleeping and I wish to sleep with her. You go to Gogo's for a while so I can rest."

"*Yebo, umama,*" Ntombi grinned.

She always loved to go to her grandmother's hut. She picked up the little figures her father had carved for her, kissed her mother and her sleepy little sister and stepped outside the hut. At the top of the homestead was Gogo's hut. Ntombi stood in its doorway.

"Look, Gogo, *Ubaba* has added an elephant and a lion to my family of animals," she said.

"Ah, yes, *inhlovu*, the mighty elephant. Such fine detail. Ah… *ingonyama*, the great lion. Your father is a skilled carver."

"Gogo, why is your hut so much bigger than all the others?" Ntombi asked, looking around the big circular space.

"It has to be bigger because I share it with the Ancestors. If you look up you will see those spoons and plates there in the rafters. We use those when we honour the Ancestors by inviting them to special occasions."

Ntombi looked up into the crisscross of wood above her head at the various carved wooden plates, spoons and bowls balancing and hanging there.

"What special occasions?" she asked.

"Like when we sacrificed the goat, inviting them to share in the celebration of Vumile's wedding, or when we sacrificed the cow when old Mbulelo died. If we left them out they would be unhappy with us and might not ask the Spirits to help us when we are in trouble. We must always respect our Ancestors for they gave us life and looked after us during their lives. They can still look after us even though we can no longer see them. But only if we tell them what is going on and invite them to be a part of all our celebrations and ceremonies. Come now, let's go to the fields to collect the corn."

Ntombi followed Gogo out into the sharp sunlight. They passed through the village and through the opening in the sturdy circle of thorn trunks that made up the boundary of their village. Once outside they continued walking down the gentle slope to where the rows of corn, sweet potatoes, squash and melons grew.

Hlwelo was sitting on the hard earth. The sun was hot. He watched as a small dung beetle pushed a ball of dung many times its size. Head down, grazing the dust, using its hind legs to roll the dried dung, the beetle marched its way backwards across the path and disappeared into the bush. Hlwelo was about to follow it, curious as to where it was going and what it would actually do with this ball of dung, when he heard voices. He looked up and saw Ntombi and her grandmother walking toward the fields.

Ntombi's arms were swinging in high arcs as she skipped around her grandmother, laughing. She was the closest he would ever get to having a friend. Only she had ever been kind to him. He wished he had been able to talk with her and be friends with her, but his shyness always made him retreat. He retreated now when he saw her. What he really wanted was to run to her and play hide and seek in the corn rows, laughing, reaching his hand out to tag her, dodging her attempts to tag him. Instead he stayed in the shadows.

Gogo pulled the soft outer sheath of the corn part way down. "See, Ntombi, this is how to tell when the corn is ready to pick. Here, this one's kernels are not quite ready. The colour is not right. This one here, this one is ready... you see the difference? You go try another and tell me what you think."

Ntombi went down the row and picked the fattest piece she could find. She felt the feathery softness of the golden threads coming from the top of the cocooned corn. She pulled back the green sheaves, revealing the plump yellow kernels all uniformly crowding against each other.

Hlwelo watched Ntombi choosing the corn. He knew how to do that. He often sat and watched undetected as the women in the fields attended to and harvested the crops. With no mother of his own, he was hungry to learn from all the mothers, to be close to them if only from his hiding place. He wanted to run out and show Ntombi how to do it, to share something with her. But she was already peeling back the green leaf and leaning her face close to smell its ripeness. He ached to stand beside her, to lean in and smell the sweetness of the corn with her, their shoulders touching. But, of course, she didn't need him to show her anything, not with her Grandmother at her side.

Gogo looked out over the veld as Ntombi walked along the rows of corn. She sat down on a stump. This morning no cloud hung in the vast blue. This village was the home of her ancestors, of her children, her grandchildren. She gazed at the open expanse beyond the fields, the light losing its softness as the sun began its rise higher into the sky. She cupped a handful of soil and lifting it to her broad nostrils, smelled its life. She said a silent prayer to *Nomkhubulwane*, thanking the Great Spirit for the earth's bounty. Looking up she saw her beloved granddaughter smelling the life in the corn. She smiled. She loved this young girl. It was as though she had always known her from far back in the deep recesses of time, long before either of them was here in the fields together.

Ntombi's face beamed as she came bounding up to her grandmother. "This one, Gogo, this one is ready, is it not?"

"Ah, yes, you are most right. Now, bring that one with you and we'll go to the drying rack. Give me your hand."

Ntombi helped her grandmother up and together they walked through the gate to the little beehive huts raised on stilts. They climbed the ladder. Ntombi watched the kernels fall from the corn as her Grandmother scraped the cob with a long sharpened stone. She had watched this many times and loved how the kernels tumbled over each other before landing in the basket. She helped spread them out evenly over the mat to dry. Ntombi giggled at the thought of the animals trying to climb the ladder to steal the corn. When they were done they both went back to Gogo's hut. Gogo reached into an old basket hanging on the wall and pulled out a handful of kernels.

"Today is the day you will learn to grind the corn yourself."

Ntombi reached out her cupped hands to receive the corn. The kernels were surprisingly light. They had turned almost white and were smaller than those she had just finished laying out.

Gogo knelt down by the big low curved stone bowl that rested near the fire pit. It was almost as wide as Gogo's hips. Its higher side was closest to her, the lower side sloped away. In the middle was a smooth rounded rock. Gogo took a handful of corn and placed it on the stone slab. She picked up the rock and holding it with both hands scooped the kernels towards her then pressed them away; her body rising up and back, bending forward slightly with each motion. She swayed and rocked back and forth with a gentle rhythm as the corn magically transformed into a fine powder.

"Now you try," she said as she moved aside.

Ntombi easily assumed her grandmother's position, having seen it so many times. She sprinkled some corn on the stone surface and picked up the rock. It was big, heavy and cool in her hand. Her movements were awkward and clumsy. Fragments of the corn scattered on the dirt floor. No fine powder emerged, just random chunks. Ntombi frowned.

Gogo giggled. "Relax. Imagine you are the wind in the grasses, moving back and forth. Close your eyes and go inside the movement."

Ntombi tried again with the image in her mind of willowy reeds by the river swaying in the evening, with the smell of night coming on. Awkwardly, her body began to move. She closed her eyes and felt the cool stone in her hands, her knees touching the earth. She heard stone scraping against corn against stone. Her body relaxed and began to move with ease. She kept moving and swaying until Gogo said it was enough. She stopped, opened her eyes and saw the pile of rough flour she had ground. She smiled, knowing that she would be a part of today's bread.

HLWELO

Hlwelo's chance to be close to Ntombi had vanished again. He was alone. He went back to his hut. It was empty. Perhaps his father was out on a hunt with the other men of the village. How he longed for the day when he would be old enough to go with him, to learn the ways of men, to prove himself capable and brave. Perhaps then he might have the courage to approach Ntombi.

The next day Hlwelo and Nyongo rose early and shared their breakfast quietly.

"I'll see you at the end of the day, Hlwelo."

And with that he smiled at the boy and left. Hlwelo cleared away the remnants of the meal and went to the isibaya. He gathered the cattle and steered them towards the grazing lands.

Mwele watched as Hlwelo herded the cattle through the veld. He knew they were headed to the stretch of grass that lay between two jagged cliffs of rock. He knew that there was only one way in and one way out. He signaled to the others to wait. They each held a switch, a long thin stretch of a willow branch denuded of its leaves. When Mwele saw Hlwelo guide the last of the strays into the sheltered space where the sweet grass awaited, he gave the silent command. They all crept forward without a sound. Mwele had forced Hlwelo to select this spot, systematically ridiculing him and chasing him from any open ground, threatening him.

"Don't ever let us see your pasty face ruining the beauty of our land when we are out here tending our cattle…. unless you want your ears cut off and your legs broken."

He loved to see the twitch under Hlwelo's left eye whenever he uttered some threat, sometimes at the top of his voice, sometimes in a menacing whisper. Mwele despised the disgusting colour of Hlwelo's skin, the smug look of defiance on his face. He wanted to wipe it off once and for all.

Mwele led the boys through the opening then held up his hand to halt them. He watched Hlwelo settle on a flat rock. He watched him drawing patterns in the earth with a stick. Mwele gave a wave of his hand and in a flurry of movement the boys surrounded Hlwelo, their whips raised high then slicing through air and skin as they landed on the boy's pale body.

Hlwelo's arms jerked this way and that in a vain attempt to deflect the blows, wincing with the sting of each hairline incision. He stood and charged at Mwele. Before he had taken three steps the boys leapt on him. They held him down, knees on his chest and arms and legs. Mwele walked over and stood towering over Hlwelo. He reached out his hand and smeared the blood oozing from Hlwelo's wounds over the white skin.

"We just wanted to see if your blood was the same colour as ours." He paused then said, "Yours is too red."

Mwele saw the defeat in Hlwelo's body and the hatred in his eyes. He laughed and spat into the white trembling face.

"Let him go," he said to the boys.

They released their grip and Hlwelo rolled to his side and stayed where he was in a crumpled heap. Thin lines of red crisscrossed over his limbs, torso, back and face. Drool fell from his mouth. His breath was harsh and quick. When he eventually looked up, the boys were gone. The cattle were ripping the grass from the earth and chewing slowly, their tails flicking from side to side, their eyes soft and distracted.

Hlwelo trembled with tears of shame, defeat and rage. He screamed his anger into the air. He was a hideous colour. He was alone with no protection from the Ancestors. The sound bounced between the rocks, the cattle looking up then resuming their grazing. His humiliation and frustration grew. Why did he remain silent whenever Mwele persecuted him? Why did he not challenge him to fight? He was sure he could beat him, even though Mwele was a formidable size. But Hlwelo knew he was faster, more agile. No, it wasn't fear of being beaten by Mwele that stopped him.

Hlwelo feared that he would kill Mwele. He wanted to gouge in his eyes, to rip out his tongue. If he unleashed his fury he didn't know if he could stop once he started. He feared the hatred inside him. It was a force that burned his body and tortured his mind. He left the cattle and walked into the veld. He didn't care about the cattle. He didn't care what his father would say. He wandered aimlessly, the welts throbbing on his skin. He stopped and sank to the ground. He held his head in his hands, his eyes squeezed shut, his throat tight. He did care what his father thought. He did care if something happened to the cattle. He looked up and saw a group of aloe plants. Hlwelo took his knife from its sheath and cut a long stalk of the plant. He skinned it as his father had taught him, and smoothed the slime over the red lines of blood all over his body. The coolness from the plant glided over the shades of purple that were forming around the cuts. He retraced his steps and settled back on the rock, but this time with his face toward the entrance to the enclosure and a pile of rocks at his feet. He would be prepared if they should return.

When the sun had lowered in the sky Hlwelo rustled up the quiet cattle and led them back through the veld to the village. He settled them in his father's isibaya, secured the wooden gate and walked down to the river. He scooped up the water and drizzled it onto his skin, hoping to take some of the stinging heat away from his wounds. He looked up and saw Ntombi watching him from up the river, a pile of washing at her side.

She had stopped when she heard him. As she watched him, she saw the thin, angry lines of colour all over his body. She rose and walked to him.

"Hlwelo, what happened to you?" she asked.

There was no reply. At first she saw the hurt in his eyes and then she saw the hatred.

"It was Mwele, wasn't it?" she said. She stepped closer and waited. "Here, let me help you."

She went to her pile of washing and brought back a piece of clothing. After rinsing it in the river she came closer still and gently pressed the cloth dripping with cool water onto the skin of his arm.

"I'm so sorry," she said. "I don't understand why he is so mean."

And she didn't understand. She didn't understand cruelty in any form. She took his hand in hers and lifted his arm high and pressed the cloth into his armpit and down the length of his side.

The touch of Ntombi's skin on his and the feel of the damp cloth along his side sent a shiver of a different kind of pain through his body. He wanted to cry like a baby, have her hold him in her arms, lay his head in her lap, curl up inside of her. Instead he bit the inside of his cheek until he tasted the salty blood in his mouth. Slowly he pulled his arm from her grasp.

"I am fine," he said, "Please don't say anything to anyone about this."

And with that he turned from the river leaving Ntombi, her cloth dripping river, her eyes spilling tears.

As Nyongo returned from his day he smelled the dinner Hlwelo was preparing and was proud of him. This boy had learned well. He could do all that is expected of young boys, and also all the things that should have been done by Jabulile as well. He was growing into a fine, competent young man. When he rounded the side of the hut, his heart stopped at the sight of Hlwelo's body crisscrossed with thin purple and red welts, clearly the result of a vicious whipping.

"What happened, Hlwelo?" he quietly asked.

Hlwelo was silent, his jaw set, his eyes straining as he stirred the meat in the pot over the fire.

"What is it, son?" Nyongo asked again, "What happened?"

"Can't you guess?" Hlwelo spat. "I am a disgusting colour and I am hated for it. And so it seems I must be punished for it."

Nyongo tasted the bitter acid of hate rise in his throat. Although life had not turned out at all how he had wished and this boy was a daily reminder of the loss of all he had desired, still he felt a sharp urge to punish whoever had done this to Hlwelo, to inflict as much pain upon them as he could.

He swallowed and said, "I am sorry, my son. There are those who do not understand and have no room for differences. I wish I could protect you from them but I cannot." And with that he went into the hut.

The next day was thankfully uneventful and when Hlwelo returned from securing the cattle in the isibaya he entered his hut with a sigh of relief. Today he felt the absence of his mother. Most days he didn't think about it, but today, he remembered seeing Ntombi with her grandmother in the cornfields, and the hollow feeling inside that often seeped through his belly returned. He longed for his mother, but at the same time he was angry. Wasn't it bad enough that she had left him as a helpless baby? But worse, she had formed him with skin a pasty pale sickening colour. He didn't understand. All he knew was that he was different. People looked at him too long, some with pity, some with disgust. His skin was strange, how could that be? Why had the Gods made him so ugly?

Hlwelo left the hut and wandered through the village.

"You know you killed your mother, don't you?"

The words ripped through the still air and into Hlwelo's body. He knew that voice. His back stiffened as he turned to face Mwele, bracing for the beating he expected to follow. But instead of the group of boys who always surrounded him, Mwele was alone, a solitary figure, his eyes narrow.

"You are a white demon child who killed his mother. Everybody knows it."

Here was his chance. Mwele was alone. Surely Hwlelo could take him, pummel him to a heap of quivering flesh as he had done so many times in his dreams. But he couldn't move, not one muscle, save for the involuntary twitching at the corner of his left eye. The words cut deeper than any beating. Could it be true? Could that explain why he was such a ghastly colour, why he had no mother, why he had such dark thoughts? Was he a demon in a human body, a *tokoloshe*?

"Just you wait," Mwele sneered, "one day I will kill you so you can't kill anyone else." He snorted a derisive laugh, turned and confidently strode away.

Hlwelo stood rooted to the spot. When he finally found his feet again, he went up the hill to find his father. He was at the fire making new spearheads. Hlwelo watched as his father piled the fire higher.

Nyongo had an easy grace about him. He moved with confidence at an unhurried pace. When the heat was just right he pushed the unfashioned piece of metal into the hot bed of coals. He waited until the glow and smell of the metal indicated the moment when it was ready to be worked by his steady hand. With tongs he pulled the spearhead, glowing red orange, out of the fire. He laid it on the flat stone and began pounding a rhythmic beat. His experience quickly revealed the form of the spear. Once its shape was complete, Nyongo plunged it into a pot of water, cooling it enough to be handled. He began the fine work of sharpening each side of the blade with sure strokes drawn across the sharpening stone. Nyongo was known throughout the village for the balance, sharpness and accuracy of his spears. When he was satisfied that the blade was complete he looked up and saw Hlwelo.

"Come, my son, it is time to continue learning the ways of the hunt. I am making a new spear for you, one for your very own. Let me measure the length and secure the head and then we will go."

Nyongo picked up the length of wood he had carved from a branch of a sleeping buffalo thorn tree and measured it against Hlwelo's height. He cut it to the appropriate length. From the fire he took a long iron spike. Its tip was red-hot. He pierced the tip into the end of the shaft, white smoke curling up over his hand as it seared into the wood. With the base of the spearhead in his other hand, he covered it with gum from the *umsululu* tree, and placed the spearhead firmly in the newly made hole. He waited for the metal and the wood to seal, then secured it by winding a strip of leather around the prongs at the side of the head and the top of the wood. With precision, he cut grooves in the shaft of the spear in a crisscross pattern to help steady Hlwelo's grip in case of sweaty palms.

Not only was Nyongo a master spear-maker, he had a keen sense of the ways of the animals and much knowledge to pass on to his son. Together they went into the veld.

"Bend your wrist like this," Nyongo said as he demonstrated the correct angle. "Now, move your feet further apart. Turn your shoulders away from the direction of your target and your head towards it. Stretch your front arm straight to shoulder height, level both shoulders, bend at your back elbow, steady the spear. Now, narrow your eyes so you focus only on that branch." Nyongo indicated the chosen target.

The muscles in Hlwelo's jaw clenched. His lips tightened. His body was rigid. He held his breath as he flung the spear. It fell nowhere near the mark his father had identified.

"I can't do this," he said impatiently.

"Yes, you can, you must practice."

Hlwelo's mind was consumed with Mwele's words.

"Why did she leave me?" he blurted out. "The boys in the village say I killed her."

Nyongo stopped, his arm falling slack by his side. It had been thirteen years since he had last touched Jabulile's dark skin, yet the memory of her was as vivid as if he had just lain with her.

"She died giving you life," he said. "It happens sometimes and no one is to blame."

"What was she like?" Hlwelo asked.

Nyongo paused, the image of the dark beauty that was Jabulile sharp in his mind.

"She had a quick and lively spirit. She had a wide smile and dancing eyes. She loved life." Nyongo instantly regretted this last statement as he saw Hlwelo's body flinch.

"I'm sorry she's gone, son, but you must not blame yourself."

"Was there something wrong with her that made me look the way I do? Am I a demon?" the boy asked.

Nyongo looked at the pasty skin of the boy's body. He had to reassure him that he was no demon, but he was not sure how much to say. He wondered if knowing what had happened to Jabulile would ease his son's distress or deepen his defiant withdrawal and anger. He decided it would be more respectful to both his son and his dead wife to speak the truth. His throat tightened again as he struggled to find his voice.

"There are people in the world that can be dangerous," he began. "It is always best to stay close to the village, especially for the women. Your mother found out the truth of this one day when she wandered far up the river to find berries. A white man found her and took her by force." He paused. "Half of you is that white man."

Hlwelo stared at his father... no, not father, then who, who was this man in front of him that he had always called father?

"Then I am not your son," he said coldly.

"I feel you as my son," Nyongo said.

"But how could you keep me knowing what you knew and seeing me so ugly?"

"You are also half her," he said quietly.

Hlwelo picked up his spear, threw it with all the force of his hurt and anger, and ran.

Nyongo recognized the same dark place in Hlwelo that he himself had carried since before his son's birth. He had fought that hatred ever since Jabulile had been taken by the white man. He could find no softness around his heart and yet he knew that to keep this bitter flame alive would not help him or his son. He saw how one vile incident gives birth to new ones, like tentacles reproducing and creeping through lives, creating new sorrows. He had seen how cruel the other children had been with Hlwelo. They didn't understand the difference in their skin, and not understanding it made them afraid. It was easier to be mean than to be frightened. Nyongo's heart was heavy with so much suffering. He felt powerless in the face of it, but he knew he must not allow this monster to fester in his son's heart and strangle any humanity inside him. He stood watching the boy grow smaller and smaller in the distance.

CEREMONY

Nyongo and Hlwelo finished their morning meal.

"Come Hlwelo, it is time to prepare you for your transition time."

Hlwelo had been dreading this. He watched as his father stroked the knife along the sharpening stone over and over until the blade was keenly sharp. He watched him slice strips of aloe into a slimy paste and felt its jelly-like consistency as his father rubbed it into his hair. He felt the swift and sure strokes of the blade over his scalp and the clumps of tight curls falling about his shoulders. Against his will, tears welled up in his eyes.

"Is it as bad as they say?" he asked.

"Everyone reacts to pain in their own way. When you think it is beyond what you can bear, remember you are stronger than you think. Call on the strength of the Ancestors. Remember, every man in the village has endured this. You will be fine."

All the boys of the village who had passed their fifteenth year assembled in front of the Chief. It was the time for them to undergo the transition into manhood. It was the time the boys both feared and welcomed, for it meant that if they were successful they would earn their place among the men of the village. They could seek a bride, they could be elected to positions of responsibility and power. But it also meant circumcision. They had heard many frightening tales of the pain involved and the possibility of infection, mutilation or death.

The Chief stood tall, his shoulders draped with leopard skin, a necklace of lion's teeth at his throat, a staff carved from a *lidloti* branch in his hand. He surveyed the gathering of a dozen boys accompanied by their fathers. Each boy's head was cleanly shaved.

"You are here today in front of your Chief as boys who have tended your family's cattle and gone through life as innocent, carefree children. It is time now to step into your power as a man. It is time for you to contribute to the life of our village as strong, courageous men capable of increasing our numbers and protecting our women and children. Your fathers stand beside you. They have undergone this rite of passage before you and have contributed to the strength and harmony of our village. They have taught and guided you throughout your fifteen years. We send you out into the wilderness now. You will return to follow in their footsteps and continue to honour and uphold the traditions of our people. Go now. Be brave. Find your strength and return as men."

Each father held their son close to their chest, the last time they would embrace them as boys. They knew what awaited them, the memory of their own transition still vivid after all the years. Each father draped a cowhide over the shoulders of his boy.

The boys left their fathers and the village, following the male elders who led them to their future. Once high off in the hills each boy in turn was instructed to find a secluded area and build himself a small shelter with sticks and branches gathered from the land.

Hlwelo watched closely to see where Mwele was setting up his space and made sure to find his own area as far from him as possible. He feared that if he cried out Mwele might hear and would forever ridicule him for not having the strength to become a man.

The terrain was wide and varied with many secluded spots. Down by the river was a large open area where the boys gathered each day, their heads bare and their bodies naked. Each day the elders spoke of the history of the *Mswembe* tribe, they shared their knowledge of how to survive in the wild and they counseled the boys on how to resolve conflict. Each night the boys returned to their solitary space to contemplate the words of the elders. Each day there was less food and less drink.

On the morning of the thirteenth day the elders sat in front of the boys. The *Induna* said, "Today we begin the next step in your initiation. You will return to your shelters and await the arrival of Bhekabantu. After his visit you may have no food, only water for seven days and seven nights. You will not communicate with each other during this time. At the end of the seven days you may once again talk. You will meet each other as men. On the second day you must bury your foreskin in an anthill. Now we will go to the river and prepare."

The boys followed the Induna to the river. They walked along the banks until their feet sank into soft white clay. They scooped up handfuls of clay and covered their bodies with a thick layer of mud.

Hlwelo felt the silky texture of the clay cool against his skin, the pleasure of it dissipating the heat of the day from his limbs. He closed his eyes and smelled the earthy wet as he smoothed it over his nose, his cheeks, around his eyes and down his neck. A hiss of sound penetrated his enjoyment.

"It makes no difference to your colour. You are not one of us," he heard Mwele's dark whisper. Mwele passed close to Hlwelo and said in a dark hushed tone, "You will never be a man. And don't think we would allow you to touch any of the women of our village, or any other village. They are for men only."

His eyes snapped open. He saw Mwele standing close by, his eyes fiercely focused on him. Hlwelo shuddered inside, but continued the ritual of applying the clay, his body now alert.

Mwele watched as all the boys smeared the clay on their bodies, transforming their blackness into white. He looked at Hlwelo. He looked at the others. There was no difference between them. A shudder passed through his body. Preparing for the initiation they all had to become white, pure in the eyes of the Ancestors, pure enough to be accepted as worthy of becoming men. Had Hlwelo been pure all along? Had he in fact been a step ahead of all of them, a Chosen One? Mwele's stomach churned and pitched. Would he be punished for having beaten and humiliated Hwlelo? He gingerly applied the paste to his own skin and quietly slunk back to his shelter.

Hlwelo returned to his shelter, the white clay drying on his white skin. He waited with his knees huddled close to his chest as he sat looking out through the opening of the branches, attentive to any and all sounds. Was that the snap of a twig, the sigh of the wind or the cry of a boy? He worried that he was not up to the task, that he would cry out the moment the knife pierced his manhood, that he would be, after all, not worthy of being called a man. Time dragged on. Had he already been overlooked? Already assessed as unworthy? And then the shadow of the Bhekabantu appeared announcing the arrival of his moment.

Bhekabantu entered the small space, his face hard, his eyes set.

"Hlwelo," he said, "son of Nyongo, are you ready to become a man?"

"Yebo, I am ready," Hlwelo said.

Bhekabantu's assistant carried with him two bowls of mixtures and a handful of long leaves.

"This is a combination of powders from healing plants mixed with honey and the crushed leaves and sap from the Buffalo Thorn tree. You must put this on your wound each day and bind it with one of these leaves. And this is a mixture of water, aloe, and dirt from an ant hill." He smeared some into the clay on Hlwelo's chest and face.

"Here, drink. It will make you strong and sturdy. It will harden your heart so you won't be a coward. Drink this so you won't get dizzy and faint like a girl."

Hlwelo sipped the silty liquid. It tasted of dirt and death. He saw the flash of the *assegai* as it appeared in the air. He felt the firm grip on his penis and then the hollow descending pain burrowing deep into his veins spreading from his groin through to every nerve in his body. He didn't flinch. He didn't cry out. His ears buzzed and his body trembled. He felt the whisper of the cowhide on his skin as Bhekabantu wrapped it around his shoulders. From what seemed like a long distance away Hlwelo heard him speak.

"The shivers will end soon. You are now a man. Say it."

Hlwelo unclenched his teeth.

"I am now a man," he said.

And then he was alone.

The blood pooled on the ground between his legs. The world spun. His mind reeled. He took a sharp intake of breath, placed his hands on the earth and steadied the ground beneath him.

"I am now a man," he said again. "I am now a man," he said again and again, trying to convince himself it was so.

He took the poultice and gingerly applied it to the exposed skin and wrapped his penis loosely in one of the leaves. In time the searing pain retreated into a relentless throbbing. He was thirsty but took only tiny sips from his water-skin. Throughout the day his body and mind passed in and out of a deranged feverishness. From time to time throughout the night he would fall into a fitful sleep only to awaken with a jolt of pain if he moved his body in any way.

The next morning, before the sun had advanced into the sky, he staggered from his lean-to, his bloodied foreskin in his grasp. All was quiet and still, save for a few birds beginning their soft trills. Hlwelo saw drops of dew within the folds of the plants. He passed them by. He walked until he found an anthill not far from his isolation spot. He dug into the side of the hill with some effort, penetrating the strong structure.

Far inside he buried his foreskin along with his boyhood and covered it over. It was now safe to be consumed by the ants, no longer exposed to the silent sorcerers who might steal it to make black *muti*, bad witchcraft.

As each day came and went, Hlwelo tended his wound, being careful when he passed water to not allow any to splash onto the raw, exposed skin. Soon he began to feel strength returning to his limbs, his breath was deeper and calmer, the delirium abating. But also as the days went on he thought he heard a low moaning sound. It haunted him throughout the daylight hours and into the dark of night and into his dreams. Was the sound coming from him? Sometimes he couldn't tell. He prayed it was just the wind bending the grasses.

At the end of the seven days, the men who were once boys were summoned from their isolation. They assembled and, on the signal from the Induna, they all charged into the river, splashing into the cool water with shrieks and laughter, drinking in the fresh water. They washed clean the caked white clay from their bodies. They washed away all traces of their childhood, swimming in their newness as men.

But where there had been twelve there were now only eleven. When they emerged from the river, trails of water streaming down their legs the Induna said, "One of you did not survive. It happens. It is part of the natural process of selection to find out who is truly a man and who is not. He shall be buried as a boy." The men were silent, all joy evaporating into the hot air.

The men remained in the wilderness for another fourteen days receiving instructions on how to live an honourable and useful life. Hlwelo maintained a distance at all times from Mwele, even as he noticed that Mwele barely looked his way and he sensed no danger from him. Was it Mwele he had heard moaning throughout the isolation time? The day arrived when the elders approached the men and greased their bodies with a thin coating of animal fat and clothed them with new loincloths. Together they made their way back to the village, their skin glistening in the sun. The villagers sang their welcome at the gates. They celebrated by smoothing handfuls of red clay over the men's bodies to declare and acknowledge their new status. Hlwelo walked among them feeling exposed and naked in his white skin. And when he and his father shared his first man's embrace, Hlwelo felt broken in a way he did not understand.

FIRE

The men of the village took turns keeping the fire slowly burning through the night; not so brightly as to waste the precious wood, but not so quiet that it would die away. Tonight was Dinzane's night. He gathered a pile of light brush and placed it by the fire in preparation for enlivening it in the morning. The season was just beginning to turn; the evening held a chill. He prayed that the coolness might bring with it some welcome rain. The dry land so badly needed to be soaked through with the liquid of life. But the smell of the air did not hold the promise of rain.

He went to his hut and picked up the wildebeest skin to keep away the chill. He kissed his Lindiwe on her sweet mouth and ran his big hand over the head of each of his adored children, giving a special wink to Ntombi, then wished them all a restful sleep. He took one last stroll around the isibaya, ensuring the animals were all gathered in and then checked that the wooden gate to the village was properly secured. The village was still but for the sound of a few quiet conversations wafting from darkened huts.

He returned to the fire pit, seating himself on the ground, drawing the skin around his back and across his shoulders. He gazed into the burning embers, comforted and endlessly fascinated by the shapes and images that appeared and disappeared. He was becoming sleepy. As the fire began to diminish, he placed a big log in its centre, one he knew would burn slowly. He settled himself, repositioning the skin over his body. Trusting that he would awaken at the right moment to check on the fire, Dinzane slipped into sleep.

Had it been daylight, Dinzane would have seen the clouds building, gathering in waves and rolling across the sky as far as the eye could see. He would have thought the Gods were now smiling on the people and sending rain to the dry earth to kiss life back into the dust. But he would have been wrong.

The air between sky and ground was hot and greedy. It gobbled the tiny droplets of moisture mid-fall, devouring their very existence before they could reach the ground, leaving no trace. Jagged fingers of light thrust their way through the dark and the heat to touch the earth. Wind, low rumblings, sparks all shaking through the night.

Had Dinzane been awake, he would have seen the village exposed in a flash of momentary light. He would have seen the glow and flames of wildfire that leapt to life in the veld under the forceful shock of light. If he had turned his face at just the right moment, he would have seen the spear of light pierce the thatch roof of a hut. He would have seen the wind hurl a flame to the next hut and the next in an angry lust for destruction. He would have seen the wind lift the flaming brush from the fire pit to the skin that covered him. But he saw none of this. He was deep in sleep.

Dinzane was dreaming. He dreamed he was walking down a steep path, enclosed on either side by high jagged walls of rock. It was dark. He was slipping on a river of sharp, loose rocks. His feet were bleeding and hot. He heard the Ancestors calling him, but could not hear what they said, only a confusing jumble of crackling sound.

Dinzane awoke trapped in a cocoon of fire. The flaming wildebeest skin melted into his skin. He screamed in searing pain as his flesh burned. Sparks flew from one roof to another, swallowing the tinder dry huts in a few gulps. Smoke and flames were spreading everywhere, people screaming, running. The animals bucked and thrashed against each other in panic, running wildly around the small isibaya, breaking through the flimsy bindings of the enclosure, the sound of their terrified bellowing adding to the shouts of the men and the screams of the women and children.

Hlwelo sat up, his nostrils full of smoke. What was going on? He heard screams and the sounds of people running outside the hut. It was hard to see anything through the thick haze. Where was father? Flames started shooting, illuminating the space around him. There lay his father on a flaming mat. Hlwelo leapt across the hut to him but the flames were too fierce. He screamed for help but all the others were lost in their own panic. He approached the flaming mass once more, thrusting his hands through the fire. He grasped his father's legs and pulled with all his young strength, dragging him outside the burning hut.

Mnani, running by, stopped and picked up Nyongo and ran, with Hlwelo running close beside him. They didn't stop until they were well away from the burning village. Mnani placed Nyongo on the ground but there was no life left in his body. In the light of the smoky dawn, Hlwelo stared at the still body of his father. Gone now was his shield, his protector, his safety. He went numb.

Over the chaos, the men's shouts tried to make sense of the madness. Mnani ran from hut to hut directing people to grab gourds, skin sacks, whatever they could find, run to the river, fill them with water and send them back to the village, passing them from one person to the next in a human chain. The villagers were frantic to contain and eliminate the fiery blanket of death covering their village. And the flames raged still higher, bled faster, spreading, seeping, jumping, and leaping. Almost the entire village was consumed. Those who could, ran to the river; stunned, crying, shouting for their loved ones, not knowing who was saved and who was destroyed.

Gogo and Ntombi

Ntombi wandered aimlessly through the veld. She had been sleeping soundly on her grass mat when she was awakened by her mother's screams and shouts, telling her to run. There was fire everywhere. She had run blindly through the smoke and heat, and now found herself in the cold, dark night. She stumbled along not daring to stop. Finally, out of the dark, the sky began to lighten. She could make out the barren bushes and the low grasses that stretched out before her. She was lost. She had no idea in which direction her village lay. She heard no reassuring voices. She saw no huts. Where was her mother? She wiped her sore and tired eyes with her fists and began to walk in the direction of the growing light.

She saw a figure off in the distance walking towards her. She trembled and looked around. There was nowhere to hide. The veld was unforgiving in its openness. She slowed her pace, willing herself invisible. The figure grew larger and larger as it approached until she could distinguish the fierce features of a Mswembe warrior. He had a spear in one hand and a small animal draped over his shoulders. Blood was dripping from its neck, trickling down over the warrior's black skin.

The figure approached her without a sound, his weathered face unreadable. She remained rooted to her spot, unable to move. He stopped a few feet away from her. She held his gaze and felt an unusual sensation moving through her body, a low buzzing sound in her ears. He took the animal from his shoulders and laid it on the ground in front of her.

It was a little steenbok, a very young one. The lifeless body began to stir. The wounds in its neck began to close. Its eyelids flickered open, the long eyelashes quivering. It moved its head and then its legs, shifting its weight back and forth. Ntombi had seen this before when she had watched newborn calves. The little antelope struggled to get its ungainly feet in a position to support its efforts to stand. Ntombi was transfixed watching this determined little animal. Eventually it stood, shaking its big ears. Ntombi could see in the gathering light its soft reddish brown fur and white underbelly. The animal turned to look straight into her eyes. As she stared into the depth of those eyes, everything disappeared and the low buzzing sound again filled her ears.

Slowly the sound receded, the landscape returned. She looked to the dark man. He raised his hand. It was missing a finger. He gestured behind Ntombi and said, "Go, she will lead you back to your people. Go, now." He turned and began to walk back in the direction from which he had come. With the sun rising on the horizon it was hard to see. Ntombi lifted her hand to shield her eyes and watched the figure slowly disappear into the sun.

The little steenbok trotted past Ntombi. She turned to follow, walking fast to keep up. She smelled smoke. She approached what was left of the village. The fire had transformed all she had known of their *muzi* into charred remnants. All was quiet except for the occasional shifting of smouldering wood and thatch. At first there seemed to be no one there. Then, gradually, she began to make out the disfigured corpses that lay scattered on the ground, their bodies twisted in the agony of an excruciating death. Numbed by sheer horror, Ntombi followed the little deer through the smoking village to the river. She saw her grandmother under the trees lying beside a number of other villagers. Was everyone dead? The deer went over to her grandmother and nudged her with his soft snout.

Gogo stirred and opened her eyes, bewildered by this small animal. Then she saw Ntombi. Her face contorted into a mixture of pain, joy, and relief. She let out a wailing sound and staggered to her feet. Running with a clumsy, unsteady gait she enfolded her granddaughter in her round fleshy body. Weeping, Gogo thanked the Ancestors for the miracle that Ntombi was alive and unharmed.

"The Ancestors have spared you, my little one, you are here, you are alive. We thought they had taken you to them as they have taken so many. But you and I remain."

"What do you mean?" asked Ntombi.

"I am sorry, my child, but your mother and father and little Bonisiwe, Lwazi and Sandile did not escape the flames."

It was as if Ntombi did not hear what her grandmother had said. "What do you mean?" she said again.

"You and I are the only ones left of our family, my child."

Ntombi's eyes went vacant, uncomprending.

"What do you mean?" she whispered.

"It seems that the fire started when sparks flew on the wind from the flashes of light in the night sky. They landed on top of the huts and burst into flames. The fire jumped from hut to hut until the whole village was on fire. With so many asleep, and it spreading so fast, not many could make their way out in time. Those of us who could, ran down to the river and tried to carry pots of water up to kill the fire, but it was too late, everything burned so fast. So many have died."

Gogo tried her best to hold her sorrow beneath her voice. Her hand felt a nudge from the wet nose of the little deer.

"Where did you find this little steenbok?"

"I saw a man out in the veld, it was like he came out of the rising sun. He was dressed like a great Mswembe warrior. He had scars on his cheeks and one of his hands was missing a finger. I was frightened. He laid this little deer at my feet. I thought it was dead as it has a big cut in his throat and there was a lot of blood. But when the man put him on the ground, the cut and the blood disappeared. He told me to follow the deer who would lead me to you."

On hearing this Grandmother grew silent and said no more. She gathered Ntombi close as if to take her inside her own body. She held her there for a long while.

Finally she said, "You will live with me now. I will look after you until you are called to do your service for the Ancestors. My life has been blessed through you."

Aftermath

Together with the other villagers Gogo and Ntombi walked back to the smouldering wreckage, trying to comprehend the complete devastation. The extent of their loss began to dawn on them all; the few who could be accounted for against the inevitable assumption that those not standing in their midst were in the charred remains before them. The grueling task of how to bury their dead hung heavy. The burial ritual had always been a time for the village to come together to comfort the bereaved. Now there were so few left to bury so many, no one was immune to the weight of grief. How to support your neighbour when you, yourself, were staggering with your own loss? Over the following days, those left alive moved as if in a trance, disconnected from anything they had known, unfamiliar with the world they now inhabited.

Hlwelo went to the Chief. Anxious and impatient, he waited to be acknowledged and for the Chief to address him. Having sprouted tall over the last year, Hlwelo stooped his shoulders out of respect so as not to appear taller than the Chief.

"*Sawubona*," the Chief said.

"Sawubona," Hlwelo replied. "I have come to ask your help to honour my dead father. I need to sacrifice a bull to assure his spirit will be safe. I need to wrap what is left of his body in its skin and bury him properly."

The Chief saw the hard glint in Hlwelo's eyes but without hesitation said, "I wish I could help you, Hlwelo. Your father was a fine man and a great craftsman. Our village is less without him in it. But with so many called to the Ancestors and so many cattle gone we would be left with none if we were to honour every lost man. We will have a special ceremony and ask the Ancestors through one collective sacrifice for the grace of the Spirits to visit all who are gone and take them to safety. I promise you, each man will be named, none will be missed. I believe the Ancestors will understand our great loss and grant our request. Nyongo will be honoured alongside all the others."

The Chief held Hlwelo's gaze, feeling the boy's resentment shooting deep into him.

"I am sorry, Hlwelo, it is all I can do for you. There are others who have come before you have with this same request and my reply to all has been the same."

Hlwelo swallowed back the bitter taste in his mouth, straightened his shoulders so he stood a fraction taller than the Chief.

"Yebo, *ngiyezwa*," he said, but he didn't understand. He turned his back on the Chief and walked away.

* * *

Gogo thanked the Ancestors for sparing her dearest friend, Gosololo, and for sparing the crops. Together, with the other remaining women, they quietly gathered the corn and the beans, then sat grinding them into flour and preparing meals for those who were left.

Ntombi stayed very close to Gogo. During the days she followed her everywhere she went never losing sight of her. From behind Gogo's wide hips she watched the other children and recognized her own pain reflected in all of them. No one had escaped the loss of a loved one. During the nights, she slept curled against Gogo's body and often woke in terror, crying out for her mother. Gogo would wind her arms around her and rock her until she fell back into a troubled sleep. Gradually Ntombi began to find her own feet again and ventured from time to time out on her own down to the river to fetch water or to the fields to bring back food for the evening meal.

The villagers set about rebuilding their homes and isibayas, walking far and wide into the veld to collect young saplings to bend into frames. They collected reeds for the thatch. They brought mud from the river to slather over the frames.

In the garden the vegetables were growing full and ripe. Any day now would be the big harvest when they would gather the food, pile it in the centre of the village and dance…. dance a celebration in gratitude to the Ancestors for successfully entreating Nomkhubulwane, Goddess of agriculture and rain, to provide for them. They would dance and sing their gratitude to *Unkulunkulu*, the Supreme God, for sparing them from the destruction of the fire. And this time they would dance for their loved ones who had now joined the Ancestors.

Hlwelo slipped into the garden enclosure. He had followed Ntombi there. He saw the ripple of movement in the corn and crouched low beside the bushes. She emerged, her dark skin shining from the efforts of her work and the heat of the sun. He waited until she was close. He saw her pause and turn to look in his direction. He stood up.

Alarm fired through Ntombi's body. Her skin prickled and she gasped.

"Hlwelo, you frightened me. What are you doing here?"

"I came to see you," he said.

"What about?" she asked.

"I don't know," he said. "I just wanted to see you."

Ntombi paused, not quite knowing what to say. She had not known how to reach out through her own sorrow to comfort Hlwelo, but she had been keenly aware of how much further inside himself he had retreated.

"I am sorry about your father," she said.

Hlwelo was quiet. He believed it was her father who was responsible for the death of his father, and yet, her father was also dead, and her mother and siblings as well. "You have also lost much," he said.

"Yes, it has been very hard." Ntombi looked at him. There was silence. Finally she said, "We don't see you very often."

"No."

"Well, perhaps we will see you at the harvest celebration. We who remain must have been spared for a reason and it is right that we should give thanks for the crops that sustain us."

"I don't see it that way. There is nothing to celebrate."

"Oh," Ntombi said, almost in a whisper. She saw the hardness in his eyes and she felt uneasy.

"I must go now," she said. "Perhaps you will change your mind and I will see you at the celebration." She turned, her fingers tightly gripping the sides of the basket full of corn, and left the garden.

As the days and months passed after the Great Fire, Hlwelo's heart grew cold and numb. A fiery ball of hate grew in the centre of his belly that burned with an intensity that frightened him at first. But he began to draw strength from this hate. He cursed Dinzane for not having prevented the Great Fire that killed his father, that destroyed so much of the village and sent so many to the Ancestors. His darkness wanted to destroy anything that hinted of beauty. He vowed vengeance.

Hlwelo lived his days in stony silence. Some of the villagers, understanding the depth of his grief, tried to comfort and help him. Even those who had always ostracized him felt a pang of regret to see him suffer so, but eventually everyone left him alone, at a loss as to how to penetrate the silence he had built around himself. He sulked his way through his days, determined in his quest to not need or care for anyone. His nights were full of the terror of a recurring nightmare: Dinzane going from hut to hut, fire shooting from his eye sockets igniting thatch. Smoke and flames billowed everywhere and Hlwelo was helpless to stop it.

He rebuilt the hut he had shared with his father, made his own fires, cooked for himself and remained apart from village life. He watched everyone, all their movements and habits. He watched and waited for a plan of action and an opportunity to show itself that would allow him his revenge.

Hlwelo watched Ntombi grow into a beautiful young woman. Her face was smooth and open with the sweetness of her nature. Her body began to change, her hips broadened, her breasts became round and full. He knew her initiation into womanhood was not far off. Her innocent smile haunted him. He hated her for what her father had done and yet, at night, he would dream of touching her, entering her. He would wake in a feverish sweat, his manhood swollen in a painful ecstasy and he would curse her for tormenting him as he worked his way to release. His breathing would slow, his body would relax and his heart would ache with the conflict of what he felt for her.

MANDLA

Mandla caught sight of Ntombi just down the river. She was bending over the washing. He saw her young slender body with its rhythmic motion kneading the clothes. He watched as one hand would arc through the air trailing little trickles of river, bringing down the smooth round rock to pound the dirt out of the cloth. He could hear her voice effortlessly singing with a sweet clarity that drifted through the distance between them, settling on him like a warm caress. He had watched her for a while now, wondering whether to approach her or just bask in the delight of the sight and sound of her. He came here often hoping to see her, unseen, when he could drink his fill of her without having to look away to cover his fascination, as happened all too often in the village. He couldn't remember when he had started to love her. It was a delicious feeling, his one warm secret that brought a smile to his lips at the most unexpected moments during the day and night. If he approached her, he ran the risk of her disinterest. Perhaps it was better to leave things as they were. And yet, he always felt suspended in a sweet pain. He fluctuated between luxuriating in the happiness he felt when he saw her and the discontent he felt when she was gone. Would today be the day he walked over to her, or would he walk away as he had done so many times before?

Ntombi stopped mid-motion, the song in her throat abruptly silent. She had felt something catch in her heart. What was it? Was it an animal in the reeds? Was it a bird overhead? Was it Gogo calling her? No, it was none of those things, but it was something, something stirring inside her and hovering in the air around her.

Mandla stopped breathing, arrested by the sight of her hand suspended high above her head, the water sliding down the length of her mahogany skin, past the indent of her underarm, skirting the roundness of her young breast, absorbing into her muted mud-cloth wrap.

Slowly Ntombi lifted her head and lowered her arm. Her eyes slowly pulled to the tree just down at the bend in the river, and there she saw him. The light played through the leaves and dappled his black body. He appeared and disappeared over and over again with the dancing light. She was mesmerized.

Mandla felt her gaze penetrate him like a hot sun. The two of them remained motionless.

Thandi, Phumzile, and Cebesile came crashing down the path, laughing and singing. Ntombi turned to them, their voices a harsh intrusion.

"Ntombi, why do you come to the river by yourself? You never wait for us!

Ntombi, never wanting to offend, smiled and merely said, "I love the gentle sound of the water and sometimes I just like to be alone with it."

The girls plunked themselves down beside her, chatting and giggling. They set down their washing bundles from atop their heads, each searched out the perfect pounding stone and busied themselves with their tasks.

When she could do so undetected, Ntombi glanced in the direction of the tree. Mandla was gone. She felt a pang of disappointment. She knew it was him, even from this distance. Lately she had begun to notice him around the village. Although they had grown up near each other all these years, she hadn't paid him any attention until recently. On more than one occasion she had had the feeling that he was watching her. But when she looked, she would see his head turning away so she could never be sure if his eyes had previously settled on her or on something else. She had taken to stealing glances at him when he was engaged in some activity. Her favourite was watching him play sticks with his brothers and friends. Watching his strong, sleek, muscled body sweating and lunging in the powerful mock fight ignited a strange, tingling warmth she had never felt before. It was an unusual, curious sensation in her woman place that made her blush. It had been him in the shadows of the tree, she knew it, her body knew it and she blushed again.

Hiding her disappointment she returned to her washing, vaguely listening to the tedious gossip that the girls insisted on as a way to pass the time. Ntombi had never been very interested, mostly preferring Gogo's or her own company.

She had been truthful when she said she loved the sound of the river. She often came there alone, even without any washing, just to immerse herself in the sweet sounds and the cool breeze that lifted off the river just when it seemed too hot to keep breathing. She loved watching the river swell with the rains of summer, the reeds grow green and full, each bird and insect calling their deep-throated appreciation of abundance. She loved the end of summer when she had finally had enough of the heat and the heavy air, always impressed at the willingness of the leaves to let go and fall back to the earth, to feed the land as it slept. She even loved the scarcity of winter, the land barren, dry and yellow-brown, the river reduced to a faint trickle, the different animals that would find their way to the precious water. And she loved recognizing the signs heralding the change from winter to spring. She could feel the anticipation of new life in the land, in the buds on the bushes, the light green shoots waiting to explode with the impending rains.

Ntombi looked toward the tree again, knowing he would not be there but looking again just the same.

All that afternoon and evening, Ntombi looked in the village for any sign of Mandla, but saw none. The next day she went back, settling herself a little closer to the bend in the river, a little closer to the tree. She sat at the edge of the water. She felt disappointment creeping up with a sad thought that perhaps she had made up yesterday's incident in her head. Suddenly her body changed, sensing his presence. She looked up and saw the same dappled light playing on his beautiful body...that body that fully reflected the meaning of his name...Mandla...power, strength. She saw it in each shaped muscle that shone in the sun. She didn't know what to do. She thought she should turn away but she longed for more of him. What was the right thing to do? The other girls would have known, they were always talking about boys. Perhaps she should have paid more attention.

"Sawubona, Ntombi," Mandla said as he stepped to the edge of the shadows.

"Sawubona, Mandla," she barely replied.

There was a long pause.

"You have no washing today."

"No," she said, and not able to think of anything else to say, said nothing more.

"You come to the river often. I have seen you many times here on your own. What do you do when you are here with no washing?"

"Mostly I sit and listen. I watch and I wait."

"What do you wait for?" Mandla asked, moving a step closer, emerging from the shade, the sun exposing the fullness of his form. She paused, caught by the sight of him, so close and radiant.

"I wait to hear the Ancestors. Gogo says they will call to me one day." She stopped, looked down and quietly said, "I'm sorry. Perhaps I shouldn't have said that."

"Why are you sorry?" he asked.

"I have never spoken to anyone about this before. It feels very…" she searched for the word, "…private. I don't know if the Ancestors will be angry with me now."

"I am happy you have shared it with me. It is not hard to believe that you are favoured by the Ancestors. You are not like the other girls with their silly ways. There is a mystery about you that I find…that I….that I like," he said, shyly.

Ntombi turned to look at him and could see the gentleness in his eyes. He was not mocking her. She felt an openness inviting her in. She wanted so badly to yield to it but her solitary, cautious nature pulled her up short and she said, "I must go now."

"I have offended you," he said.

"No!" she said too quickly and too loudly, turning towards him. She halted, "It's just that… I must get back to Gogo. I have been gone a while and she may need me."

With that she turned and walked away from the river. Mandla watched her shape recede down the path. He felt confused and frightened that he had said something wrong and that now she would avoid him. He cursed himself for not having stayed silent in the shadows.

THE BEADED NECKLACE

Over the next couple of days Ntombi was quieter than usual.

"What is it, my girl?" Gogo finally asked.

"What do you mean, Grandmother?" Ntombi replied, startled out of her thoughts.

"There is something on your mind, something troubling you."

"Oh, it is just a bit of nervousness about my upcoming isolation time," Ntombi fibbed.

Gogo's eyes narrowed and she smiled.

"I think not," she said. "I suspect your thoughts are dwelling on something else…some young man, perhaps?"

Ntombi exhaled audibly and shook her head. "How is it that I can never keep anything from you? How is it you always know what is in my heart?"

"It is just so, my girl. Tell me."

"I am confused, Gogo. I feel strange when I am with him. I saw him the other day by the river, and…and…I told him I am waiting for the Ancestor's call…I'm sorry, I didn't mean to, it just came out without my thinking…"

Gogo was touched by her granddaughter's distress and her clear respect for the Ancestors. "Did he laugh when you told him?"

"No, Grandmother, he was generous with his praise of my connection with them."

"Well, I believe he sees you clearly, child. I think you need not worry. Which boy of the village is he?"

"He is Mandla."

"Ah, yes, he is a fine young man. His father is a clever hunter and his mother is known for shaping beautiful pots."

Ntombi was comforted by her grandmother's words.

Timidly she ventured, "May I see him again?"

"Would you like me to get you some beads?" Gogo grinned with a twinkle in her eye.

Ntombi smiled for the first time in days, relieved that the struggle with her feelings had been put to rest.

"Yes, please, Grandmother," she said lowering her eyes.

Ntombi set about carefully selecting the colours of the beads to convey the correct message in the necklace for Mandla.

On the fifth day Mandla came again to the river, as he had every day, hoping to see Ntombi. He told himself if he did not see her today he would know that he had offended her beyond measure, and he must resolve to banish any further thoughts of a possible future with her. He sat in the shade of the tree, dejectedly pushing a stick in the sand, drawing designs, scratching them out and redrawing random patterns. He paused, sensing her. He turned and looked up behind him to see Ntombi standing there, smiling. He felt a shiver of delight pass through him as he slowly stood up to face her.

"I am glad you have come," he said. "I was afraid you did not want to see me again. I'm sorry if I spoke wrongly to you the other day. I meant no disrespect."

"No, I just needed some time to think. This is a bit difficult for me as I know I am not following tradition correctly. I have no sisters now and no real girl friends to deliver this for me, so I am taking a chance and giving this to you myself, in person, now, before I lose my nerve and run away."

She felt foolish, she was afraid she was talking too much and he would perhaps think her silly after all, like the other village girls, and change his mind about her.

She held out the small beaded necklace with its delicate pattern of white, black, green, blue and red. She relaxed when she saw his eyes opening wide as he grinned. She saw the light colour of his upturned palm as he held it out to receive her gift. She deposited the necklace, her fingers brushing against his as she withdrew her hand.

"Tell me its message," he said, running his finger over the beads.

Pointing to the black beads she said, "This is for the rafters inside the hut we might one day share, blackened by the warmth of the fire. Green is telling you that I will become as thin as a blade of grass, unable to eat until we are together again. Blue is for the loneliness I feel when I am not in your presence. The red is my blood that carries the love I feel for you, and white is for the goodness and purity of that love."

"It is official then," he said. "We are together."

She smiled up at him as he stepped closer towards her. He lowered his head. She could feel his breath.

"Is it all right?" he asked.

She nodded and then felt the softness of his lips on hers.

They sat by the riverside for a while holding hands. He had long, thick fingers, his nails a pale oval against his dark skin. His hands were strong and firm as he held her hands in his. She felt safe and secure.

"The only other person who knows of this is my beloved Gogo. Would you mind very much if we keep this to ourselves for a while? I want to hold on to this feeling for as long as I can, and I am afraid it will change somehow when it becomes part of the village gossip."

"If it makes you happy then I am happy."

"Thank you," she said. "For now then, just the two of us will hold this precious feeling."

"But I am anxious to have you for my wife. How long must we wait?"

"At least until after my transition time. Then I will go about it the traditional way. I will dance at my celebration and choose you. I will fashion another necklace and get Cebesile, Thandi, and Phumzile to deliver it to you. I will act all nervous wondering if you will accept and you can act surprised and delighted!"

They both laughed at the thought of it.

"Come, let's have a race through the river to see who can reach that branch first," Mandla said.

Ntombi laughed and launched into the river, immediately falling in her haste to begin. Ntombi held up her hand.

"Wait, wait, I didn't have my balance. Let's start again." She was laughing, water streaming all around her.

Mandla laughed, "All right", he said, "This time no excuses."

They both took their stance, eyes on the branch that was extending out over the river, then eyes on each other, then eyes back to the goal.

"Ready?" "Ready." "Now!"

They splashed their way over the rocks, stumbling, regaining equilibrium, splashing at each other. Ntombi felt her body push against the river with each stride, her muscles working. It felt good. The water was a cool relief from the day's heat. She saw Mandla pushing ahead. How could she ever have agreed to such a game? Of course, it wasn't about winning, it was about joy and abandon, being together, loving one another here in the wetness of the river.

Mandla's foot caught on a root submerged in the river and he fell face first into the water.

Ntombi shrieked with delight and picked up her pace, seeing the possibility. She pressed onward, forward, closer, closer. Her breath came in gasps between giggles. There was the branch a few strides away. She turned to see how far ahead she was. She saw Mandla thrashing wildly through the water fast approaching. She pushed forward and as she reached her hand out to touch the branch, Mandla's arms encircled her from behind pulling her on top of him and under the water.

They surfaced spluttering and coughing. He held her at arm's length until they both regained their breath. His eyes shining, he pulled her close and kissed her. Her body pressed into his, joy and fullness flooding her every limb. They lingered there in the water, feeling each other's heartbeat.

They moved to the bank of the river and sat together, the heat of the sun drying them. Mandla fashioned a heart in the sand with a stick. Ntombi placed her hand over his and guiding their hands together created another heart encased in his big heart.

"I should go," Ntombi said quietly. "Thank you for this love." Ntombi left him at the river and made her way back to her hut.

Gogo was delighted to hear that Mandla had happily accepted the love letter, and agreed that she would keep their secret safe. Gogo and Ntombi spent their time with Gosololo preparing for her rite of passage. The two elder women assured the younger that there was nothing to be afraid of, that it was a joyous time of transition in which the Ancestors rejoiced to recognize her as a woman, a responsible and valuable member of the tribe.

As was the custom, Gogo, Gosololo and the other women elders of the village sat with Ntombi each day sharing their knowledge, passing on advice on all manner of things. In moments of quiet Ntombi reflected on all she had heard.

The night before Ntombi was to go into seclusion she waited until Gogo was asleep and quietly slipped out of the hut into the night. The moon was high and bright, and under its guiding light she walked far out into the open savannah, drawn ahead by an unknown call. At first Ntombi thought she heard the rustle of the wind as it shimmied through the grass. But the air was still and pressed against her face the way her mother's hands used to press against her cheeks. It was her mother's whisper, soft and low, filling the night. Ntombi looked to the west; the stars began to whirl in a dance of light. Her father's voice joined, the sound rich and full, her sister, her brothers, a chorus of murmurs growing, swelling to a wailing song sung by all the lost villagers calling to her, entreating her to help them find their rest. Ntombi wept. How could she heal her village? How could she dissolve the horror of their deaths and restore the light? The sound surrounded her, vibrating through her bones until she thought she would shatter.

"Help me," she called, lifting her arms to the night sky. All the voices gathered into one sound, clear, pure, and strong. A glow radiated far and wide, illuminating the whole veld. A cool wind blew, soothing her fever. The light dissolved, the sound ceased and she sank to the ground.

Mandla stood for a long time watching Ntombi's silhouette in the night. He heard her cry. "Help me," she had said with her arms outstretched. He wished she was calling to him but she wasn't. She was seeing things, hearing things that were for her only. He took a few steps toward her, willing her to turn to him. He took a few steps back knowing he must not intrude. He trembled, his body straining to run to her, his awe of her holding him back. He saw her crumple to the ground. His body lurched forward. He pulled back. He waited. She was so still. A warm sensation entered his forehead and swept in waves down his arms and legs. He sat on the ground. A calm entered his body and made all else fall away. A gentle sound moved through him. Once the stars had moved in their journey through the night to the edge of dawn, the sound subsided. He rose and went to Ntombi. He knelt down beside her and stroked her cheek. Her eyes opened and, seeing him, her face softened. She reached out her arms, this time it was for him.

"I don't understand," he said.

"Neither do I," she said.

Mandla lay on the ground next to Ntombi, gathering her into his arms. She rested her head on his shoulder breathing in the smell of him, the smell of strength, of earth, of life. They lay still together.

"Do you feel fear when the voices come?" Mandla asked.

"I used to. Each time I am less afraid but still I feel sad. Grandmother knew these things would happen before they began. She tells me there is no need to be afraid or sad, that I am not alone. The Ancestors are with me and will guide me."

"You are a Chosen One," Mandla said softly.

"I do not wish to be."

"But you are, and wishing it away will not change it."

"I know," she said.

Mandla rubbed his hand over her head, his fingers feeling the strong coils of her hair.

"I am frightened by the love I feel for you," he said. "It is beyond my body and my heart. It feels bigger than you and me together, and sometimes I fear it will break me."

Ntombi placed her hand on his chest. She watched her long fingers move with each beat of his heart.

"Must we wait until after your transition ceremony?" he asked.

"You know we must."

"I know," he said, and yet against his will, his manhood stirred.

In the soft light of dawn, Ntombi saw the leather cover moved aside by his growing magnificence. Her mouth opened, a quick sound of desire escaping with her breath. She sent up a silent call to the Ancestors for strength.

"I must go," she said.

"I know," he said. "I'm sorry. Sometimes my body does not obey me."

Ntombi giggled, "I'm lucky, my body keeps my desire a secret."

She kissed him, her eyes open, her gaze met by the softness of his eyes, her mouth by the softness of his lips. She rolled over and touched her forehead to the earth, thanking the Great Mother for keeping them safe.

"I will wait and enter the village from a different direction," he said.

"Thank you," she said, then added, "my love."

HLWELO

Hlwelo saw Ntombi enter the village just as the light was beginning to overpower the dark. What had she been doing out in the veld? At that moment, he knew the form his revenge would take. For weeks he had been watching the preparations for the coming of age rituals that would welcome Ntombi into the ranks of the women of the village. The women had been bustling about her, bathing her, braiding her hair, making new clothes that would reflect her new status. He knew all in the village loved Ntombi. How could they not? Everyone looked out for her and Gogo. He knew many young men pinned their hopes on having her as a bride one day.

Tradition dictated that after the first moon cycle a young girl was to spend a full moon cycle in a secluded hut, left alone to open herself to the wisdom of the ancient mothers. They would infuse her with knowledge and insight for her transition from girl to woman. She was not allowed to leave the hut for any reason other than to wash and relieve herself in an adjoining enclosed area. Specially prepared food blessed by the Sangoma would be left outside the hut for her after sunset and before sunrise, along with fresh water for drinking and washing.

Hlwelo watched and waited. On the twelfth night he fulfilled his plan. When the half moon had slid in an orange haze below the horizon, he made his approach. All was dark, but he knew every step of the way. Silently, he entered the hut. Once inside, the slightest sound of his breath escaped his lips. He heard Ntombi stir in the dark. He froze, hoping she had not noticed. He sensed her alertness, could now just begin to make out the outline of her body; then he lunged, clasping his hand over her mouth. He could feel her struggling for breath. He laughed a low sneer at the thought that she might fear she would be killed. He would not allow her terror to be done as quickly as death would allow. He wanted to beat her and crush every bone in her body. But the smell of her and the feel of her aroused him, and he felt the agony of his desire for her. His endless dreams of having her flooded him. He roughly pushed her legs apart and forced his way into her, with each thrust his feelings leaping from exhilaration to hate, to fear, to desperation, to longing, to fury. His body arched for a moment and he collapsed, spent, on top of her.

Finally he lifted himself from her, hesitated in a moment of confusion, and then hit her hard across the mouth, saying, "Now, you can belong to no one."

And he laughed, knowing she would forever carry within her the pain of what he had done.

On the way back to his hut, Hlwelo's stomach began to heave. He retched and retched, his body shaking with violent spasms. He found his way to his hut, his mind spinning, his body churning. He grabbed his spear and water skin and stumbled from the village out into the black night. He started to run a slow, rhythmic pace that gradually quickened. He ran until his legs would no longer carry him. He crumpled to the ground and began to wail, torn by his anguish. Then he grew very still. A coldness came into his body. He stood up. With no expression on his face and no feeling in his heart he walked on.

Ntombi

It had started with the smallest sound that could be perceived. So small that Ntombi wasn't even sure she had heard it. It could have been her imagination, yet every fibre of her being tensed. Her eyes opened wide, hoping to see something, anything that might give a harmless explanation for the sound. She saw nothing in the darkness but the faint outline of the opening to the hut. She strained her ears to listen, pulling all the focus she could to the detection of sound. But the harder she focused, the louder become the sound of the blood rushing in her ears. She tried to quiet her body and convince herself that she had heard nothing, that there was no reason to have such fear, to have such a desire to scream out. Then the hand clamped over her nose and mouth. She couldn't breathe. As she struggled, the fingers of the hand shifted and air rushed into her nostrils. She tried to scream but the hand held fast over her mouth, stifling any sound that would have traveled far enough to alert anyone. Then came the low growl that stopped her cold. She ceased to struggle. Her body grew still. She knew there was nothing to be done but submit to the will of whatever creature this was that had her in its grip. The intruder's body now heaved its weight over her, pushing one leg apart from the other. A hand fumbled and found her most secret and tender place, ripping at the soft hair that covered it. And then came that low, guttural laugh, slow and menacing, followed by the flash of pain. Again and again her flesh tore. With a strangled moan, the motion stopped and the full weight of his body collapsed onto her. As he lifted himself up his limpness fell out of her. And again that low growled laugh. He struck her hard on the face.

"Now, you can belong to no one," he said, his breath like hot coals on her face.

She felt the lightness of the air on her skin and a burning at the core of her body as she watched the shadow pass through the opening of the hut. She rolled to one side, and pulled her knees close to her heart. The warm mixture of blood and semen oozed from her wounded woman place into the indifferent night.

She lay there for a long while. With the light of the dawning day, willing herself to rise from the stained mat, she moved for the first time. Her limbs ached. She stumbled out of the hut and went to the water. She filled the clay pot and squatted over it. Flames licked her insides. Her hands trembled as she cupped the cool water and raised it to her torn body. The bloodied water trickled down her thighs to the earth. Ntombi watched the pools of liquid hover before disappearing into the ground. She must try to wash clean what had happened, to remove any trace, as if removing it could take her back in time to yesterday when she had been whole. But she was now broken and there was no possibility of repair. Her limbs were stiff, her body raw at its centre, the memory of the night radiating through every cell.

For the next two weeks fear would rise and her body would tense, a burning spreading below her belly. A jerking shudder would pass through her. It was like the time in her childhood when she had a fishhook deeply embedded in her finger…she had had to pull it out, it was the only way and yet it ripped her flesh open. Was there no way to mend without first being torn open again? She thought she had healed. There was no more bleeding or pain when she passed water, and for days at a time she would have some relief, only for the burning to return again when she least expected it. And who could she tell? How could she ever speak of what had happened? She would be banished, disgraced. Ntombi's thoughts were consumed with Mandla. Now he would despise and reject her. He could never know. What mattered now was that she find a way to bury this memory in her body.

* * *

When the women came to welcome Ntombi back into the village after her seclusion, Gogo and Gosololo noticed the change. Had the Ancestors taken her deep into transformational trances in her seclusion? Gogo knew beyond a doubt that Ntombi had been chosen as a future healer, but was it to happen so soon, when she was still so young? That would be unusual, but possible. Her freshness and youth seemed to have disappeared. She was quiet and withdrawn.

"I do not feel ready yet for the celebration, can we wait for a little while?" Ntombi asked Gogo.

"Yes, my girl, you let me know when you are ready." Gogo replied, feeling uneasy. This was the first time she could not read her grandchild.

Ntombi picked up the empty water jug and left for the river.

The day was warm as Gosololo and Gogo sat in the sun sorting beads into piles of pleasing colours. Gosololo watched as Ntombi left through the gate of the village. "A man's seed has been planted inside Ntombi," Gosololo said.

Gogo looked up at her friend, her breath held for a moment, then said, "It is not possible."

"It would seem not, but I know it is so."

Gogo remained silent for a while then said, "Is that what changed in her isolation time?"

"It must be so, as we both knew her nature and her movements before." "I pray you are mistaken," said Gogo. She said nothing of Mandla.

Gogo would watch Ntombi closely over the coming days and wait until the right moment to say something, but not quite knowing what.

Ntombi walked to the river, head down, feeling the pain in her body, oblivious to her surroundings. Suddenly she looked up, straight into the eyes of Mandla. Her stomach lurched. She saw the love and anticipation glowing in his eyes. Feeling the sting of tears in her own eyes, she lowered her gaze and quickly walked away. He called after her but she ran. Then she slowed, knowing she could not just run away. She turned to face him.

He came towards her, his face twisted with confusion.

"Ntombi, what is it? Why do you run from me?"

"I cannot tell you why but we cannot be together," she blurted.

"What are you saying? How can this be? We love each other, don't we?"

"I love you more than I know how to hold. I cannot explain, but I can never be your wife."

"What happened in your time away? Did the Ancestors come to you? Did they tell you I would not be a worthy husband? Why would they tell you such a thing? My devotion to you is true and strong. I am a good man and I will make you happy in our life together."

"I know you are a good man. This has nothing to do with you. You must never think that. If you love me at all, please question me no further. You must forget our love and find someone who will be good to you. I must go now."

Mandla watched Ntombi walk away. Ripped into jagged pieces and scattered in a million directions, by turns he felt numb, cold, hurt, hot, angry. A raw ache filtered through every muscle and limb. As if sleepwalking, he went out into the veld to try to make some sense of what had just happened.

Ntombi ran to the river and waded in.

The water reached to her thighs. She felt the cold bite of the river. She welcomed its sting. She needed to be shocked back into her body. The hurt on Mandla's face had sent her spiraling into a web of pain. She couldn't escape it.

What had she done to make the Gods punish her so? She cupped her hands and scooped the river up to the heavens and sent it showering down over her troubled face and her hot tears. Her knees buckled and she sank down into the river, the cold shelf of water closing over her head. Her eyes opened wide, she lifted her head out of the water, gulped a huge breath and thrust her head under and screamed into the river. Over and over she came up for air and over and over she returned to the depths to release her sorrow, her anger, her confusion. Finally she struggled to the riverbank and lay huddled in a ball, helpless in the familiar wave she felt engulfing her. She wanted to cry out for Mandla but he must never know, no one could ever know. She had to turn away the man she loved, who had held the promise of her future. She had to will her way through this and push it aside.

When the sun had lowered in the sky, Ntombi walked back to the village and entered the hut. Gogo was seated with her beads creating a magnificent necklace. Ntombi made no attempt to hide her tears. Gogo put down the necklace, went over to Ntombi, encircled her with her loving arms and said, "What is it, my girl?"

"It is over with Mandla," she said.

"What happened, child?" Gogo asked as she held Ntombi.

"It doesn't matter now. It is done." Ntombi kissed her grandmother's cheek. Removing herself from her arms, she curled up on her mat facing the wall.

Gogo knew it was not the time to say more. She covered Ntombi's small frame with a skin blanket. Her heart felt the heaviness of her beloved granddaughter's pain. She went to sit outside the hut and looked into the dull light of the fading day.

Just when Ntombi thought enough time had passed and her mind and body might begin to settle, she realized there was still no blood, the good kind of blood, the kind that had initiated her into her full potential as a woman. Even though at times this blood had brought its own sort of pain, it had been a bittersweet pain. When she was a little girl, Gogo had told her it meant that one day she would be a woman and know the joy of babies. Why was there still no blood? In the transition hut she had thought perhaps it held back out of respect while she was being held in the sacred space of the Ancestors. She shivered at the thought that a baby might have been planted inside her. Surely the Gods would not punish her for succumbing to the brutal strength of the stranger? She waited and waited, but still no blood came. She knew she must talk to Gogo.

After the evening meal, Ntombi cleaned the wooden plates and placed them in the corner ready for the morning. She came to sit beside her grandmother. In as unconcerned a voice as she could summon she said to her, "Gogo, there is something different with my body." Not able to look at her grandmother she looked down at her fingers as their tips pressed against each other.

"In what way?" Gogo asked, a wave of fear raking across her chest.

"My moon cycle has not come."

Gogo's heart sank. "Something has happened, my girl, what is it?" She looked at Ntombi gently and waited.

Ntombi felt Gogo's eyes on her. She knew she could not lie to her grandmother but she could not find her voice.

"Something happened in your seclusion time, I think," Gogo said. "Gosololo and I have both noticed a change in you." She paused. "Gosololo says there is a baby growing inside you… and now I also believe this is so. What happened?" Gogo asked softly.

Ntombi's body trembled as she finally allowed the secret of that brutal night to be told.

"I …," Ntombi stammered, "it was too dark, I could not see."

Gogo felt a rush of relief. So, it was not Mandla; she had been correct in thinking him a worthy man, but relief was quickly replaced with fear. If not Mandla, then who, and worse, how? She looked at her granddaughter and the pain she saw on her face confirmed her worst suspicion.

"Oh, my sweet child. I am so sorry."

She held Ntombi close in her arms, and felt the trembling terror that reverberated through her granddaughter's slender body. Gogo took Ntombi's face between her worn hands.

"We will call on the Ancestors to guide us through whatever may come," she said. And again she held her precious granddaughter tight against her.

Gogo kissed Ntombi on her forehead and went to sit outside in the darkening light. Now there would be no ceremony, no celebration. There would be disgrace and exclusion. Gogo wept. She remembered so clearly the celebration for the coming of age of her dearest Lindiwe. What a feisty girl she had been and what a good choice she had made in Dinzane. Gogo had never stopped grieving the loss of her daughter. She had poured all her love and hopes into Ntombi; she was all she had left. And now they were to be denied the joys of rituals, of happy births, of ordinary day-to-day life. There would be no comfort of community. They would live on the fringe, barely tolerated. Life had not in any way turned out as she had expected.

As the time passed, Ntombi's belly began to swell and it was clear to all that she was carrying a child. Where there had once been friendly greetings from everyone who passed, there were now hushed whispers or silence. And, of course, any young man who had hoped to wed Ntombi was no longer interested. Only Gosololo remained close to Ntombi and Gogo.

One day Ntombi was making her way to the river. There in the path in front of her was Mandla. She lowered her eyes and walked by. She continued to the river and set about doing the laundry. She stopped, feeling him behind her. She stopped her washing, sighed, and stared straight ahead over the rippling river.

"So, now you understand why I could not be with you. At the time I did not know I had a child growing in me, but I knew even if there wasn't and I didn't say anything, you would have felt the difference in me that would have made your heart retreat. I could not bear the thought of it."

She turned around to look at him. There were tears in his eyes and quietly he turned and walked away.

Mandla's heart was broken. How could she have done such a thing? How could he have been so wrong about her? He tortured himself with thoughts of her in another man's arms, not comprehending why she had not waited for him. He went over and over it in his mind until finally a sharp thought pierced its way through his agony... she had been taken against her will. It was the only acceptable explanation. His body knew her to be true and kind. This was the only possible explanation. He sat with this thought until every cell in his body rang with the truth of it.

He returned to the river.

"Why do you come again?" Ntombi said, "Is it to punish me?"

"I know you were taken against your will," he said.

She stopped and slowly turned around, "Why would you say that?"

"I know it in my bones," he said gently.

She closed her eyes willing herself not to cry.

Mandla stepped forward and put his arms around her. They both began to weep.

"I will marry you, he said, "I love you."

She felt such a deep love for this gentle soul and wished to the depth of her being she could accept his offer.

Instead she said, "I could never allow it. You would be falsely accused of disobeying tradition by loving me this way before we were married. You and your good family would be dishonoured and shamed. I cannot share this burden with you. But know that I love you even more for your willingness to still love me. But it cannot be. My heart has eased now you know the truth. I could not bear to have you think I would willingly be with anyone but you. You will always have my heart and I will always be grateful to you."

She took his big beautiful hands in hers, kissed each one, then returned to her washing.

"Please go now."

Mandla stood for a while looking at Ntombi's strong back. He ached to touch her. Instead he walked away.

* * *

"I keep having the same dream," Ntombi said.

Gogo looked at her carefully. "What happens in your dream?" she asked.

"There is always the same woman. I am not sure who she is, but I am wondering if she was your mother."

"What is it that makes you think that?" Gogo asked.

"In the dream she always comes to the hut. You are in the dream, too, and you bow to her in respect and she touches your cheek with a loving smile on her lips. She takes me from the hut and leads me out of the village through the veld to the rocky ledges. She shows me how to recognize and harvest all sorts of plants I am unfamiliar with."

"Yes, my girl, that is your Great Grandmother. She was a powerful and kind Sangoma. She is passing her knowledge on to you in the dream time. She recognizes your connection to the Ancestors."

"The third time I had the dream she pulled aside a skin that was covering the upper part of her body and a light seemed to shine from a necklace she was wearing. It felt very familiar although I don't think I have ever seen it before."

Gogo got up slowly and went to a small leopard skin sack hanging on the wall.

She opened it with great care and brought out the contents. Coming back to sit next to Ntombi, she opened her hand. Ntombi saw the necklace from the dream, a large amber pendant with a perfectly intact tiny dung beetle suspended in its middle.

"This belonged to your Great Grandmother. One day it may be yours to wear." Ntombi saw the tears in her grandmother's eyes.

"I pray that I may find my way and earn the right to wear it one day," Ntombi said softly.

DOYENNE

When the baby's time came, Gogo and Gosololo were at Ntombi's side, massaging her, wiping away her sweat, mixing a brew of herbs. Outside, the rain fell in a soft mist. It was a quiet and easy birth but there was no joy or singing when the little girl of the wrong colour arrived. She was small and barely made a whimper, as though not wanting to be more of a burden than was already upon these good people.

The pale colour of the baby's skin told Gogo and Gosololo that Hlwelo had been the father. Gogo thought back and remembered that he had left the village before Ntombi's seclusion time was complete. She did not question it at the time, thinking with a sense of relief, that he had finally abandoned the village he seemed to hate so much. But now she understood why he had left. She was quiet as she held Ntombi and said silently to herself, "May he walk in misery and torment for the rest of his days as punishment for what he has done."

They named the child Doyenne... rain.

Ntombi kept to herself, going about her daily chores, relying on Gogo to look after the baby when she needed to go out to fetch water from the river or firewood from the savannah. She did not want the villagers to see Doyenne, or to feel the judgment that would be directed at them both. Doyenne was unmistakably Hlwelo's child. She feared the predictable response, having seen for years how Hlwelo had been isolated. But she knew that she could not protect her child forever from the narrow minds of some who did not have room in their hearts for differences.

The sun was high in the sky. It was hot, stiflingly hot. Today was the day that Ntombi ventured out of the hut with Doyenne. She felt the small, warm body nestled close against her back, secured with the cloth Gosololo had lovingly woven for her. Dear Gosololo, always there with an open heart and open arms. Ntombi walked through the village feeling the eyes of scorn burning into her. She had Doyenne well covered. No one other than Gogo and Gosololo had seen her yet.

She made her way to the river, settling further upstream than she normally did. She tenderly swung Doyenne to the front of her body and unwrapped her. It was important to Ntombi to bring Doyenne to the river, to introduce her to its rippling sound and bathe her in its cleansing water, to introduce her to the miracle of water that was part of her name. She looked into the strange green eyes of her baby and ran her hands over her pale skin. She loved this child. How could she not? She was of her own body. Knowing how this innocent child would be shunned, she thought of how lonely it must have been for Hlwelo. Even though he had stolen her hopes of happiness, of love and life with Mandla, she had a small place in her heart of softness towards him.

She waded into the river holding Doyenne close to her chest. As the water reached the baby's feet Doyenne's face registered a look of bewilderment. As they went deeper Doyenne smiled, her face alight with the wonder of this new sensation.

"I have to trust what was given to me," Ntombi thought. Closing her eyes, she smelled the newness of life she held in her arms, felt the downy softness of the colourless skin and drank in the soft sound of her baby's laughter.

Cebesile, Thandi and Phumzile had followed Ntombi to the river. Their curiosity could no longer be contained. They each felt a gnawing guilt at having kept away from her during her pregnancy. But how could they have remained friends? They had felt deeply betrayed when Ntombi had all of a sudden become withdrawn, and then it had become clear why. Why had she not confided in them, come to them? They had suffered from the loss of their friend and they had now come to see what had taken her from them.

Cebesile was the first to see. Her eyes widened. She held her breath then let it go with a barely audible groan. Thandi and Phumzile stopped and stared. It explained so much. The girls stood rooted. Ntombi slowly turned to face them, her eyes steady, looking from one to the next. There was not a breath of wind, nothing stirred. Cebesile began to cry seeing her friend holding a lifetime of misery in her arms. She didn't know whether to run to her or run away. Finally she took one step forward and stopped, staring, mesmerized by the baby's green eyes.

Doyenne looked up at her mother's face then followed her gaze to Cebesile. Doyenne held her gaze unsure, then her face softened into a smile.

Cebesile looked at Ntombi and managed a tentative smile. She walked wordlessly into the river until she stood face to face with Ntombi.

"I didn't understand, but, of course, now I do. I'm sorry."

She was sorry for having deserted her friend, she was sorry that Hlwelo was the father. She was sorry that bad things happened. She was sorry that their carefree youth was now lost. She put her arms around Ntombi and gently hugged both her and the small baby that nestled between them.

"I'm so sorry," she said again. And both she and Ntombi cried together, the cool water of the river softly diverting around their bodies as it made its way downstream.

They all walked back into the village together. Doyenne was once again secured on Ntombi's back but Ntombi no longer covered her face. As they walked past the huts people stopped what they were doing to stare and whisper.

The Chief watched as Ntombi entered the village surrounded by Thandi, Cebesile, and Phumzile. For the first time he saw the baby, he saw the pale skin. The shock of recognition pierced his chest. His heart sank. In the preceding months he had not understood Ntombi's growing belly, as he had believed her to be a gentle girl who respected the traditions of their people. He had judged himself for being so wrong about her and judged her for being so deceitful. But here was the truth, and now he only judged himself.

This had been his fault. After the fire, all the people of the village united in their grief, for no one was untouched by its devastation, but not Hlwelo. The Chief had watched the grim set of his mouth, the hardness in his eyes. He saw the isolation, he knew of the nightly wanderings. The Chief had called on the spirits of Nyongo and Jabulile to intervene, to soften their son's hatred, for it seemed as if everything Hlwelo saw he despised. The Sangoma had warned him, but the Chief himself had not stepped in, had not taken the place of the father that Hlwelo had needed. And when Hlwelo disappeared the Chief had been relieved, glad that the problem had been resolved so easily. But, of course, it had been too simple, and now, nine months later the Chief knew that he had failed,

failed to protect Ntombi, failed to help Hlwelo find a way through his grief. Yet, how could he have known the depth of savagery that brewed inside Hlwelo? How could he have known that Hlwelo would exact such a brutal payment for Nyongo's death? No, he should have known. Many times he had seem Ntombi's attempts to include Hlwelo when the others shunned him. Many times he had seen the longing in Hlwelo's eyes, the tightness in his body when she was near. He should have known Hlwelo would go after her. If only he had acknowledged the depths of misery in Hlwelo's soul. If he had, he would have known how deep the break would be. If only he had stepped in, Ntombi would still be clean.

The Chief turned and walked back into his hut, his heart tight.

* * *

As time went on, there was a softening towards Ntombi and Doyenne. The villagers knew the burden that Ntombi carried was a heavy one. Doyenne grew into a playful little toddler with an inquisitive spirit.

She sat with Gogo in the hut. She looked at the dazzling collection of beads in front of them, watching as Gogo's hands threaded bead after bead into the necklace she was working on. Doyenne reached out to touch the pile of beads. Gogo gave her some to play with and watched as her great granddaughter arranged them into impressive shapes and designs. Both were delighted. Doyenne looked up and realized her mother was out of sight. She had a moment of panic. Her tiny feet propelled her up and out of the hut. Then her small cheeks filled with joy. There was Ntombi standing by the fire pit stirring the embers back to life. Doyenne rushed to her mother, eyes twinkling. She wrapped her fat fists around Ntombi's ankle. Looking up she giggled.

Ntombi leaned down and, with her easy way, swept her strangely beautiful daughter up through the air to land on the perfect ledge her wide hip provided.

"Come, my little one, let us go down to the field and pick some corn."

Together they waved to Gogo and made their way down through the village and through the gate to the fields. Here Ntombi had learned from her grandmother and now she would teach her daughter. She thought of how life changes so much in ways one could never imagine and yet some things remain the same. The corn grew in the same way, the earth was still the earth even though it changed from season to season, the river was still the river even though the water was never the same water that flowed past. Strange how underneath there was some sort of current that connected everything, even as life appeared to unfold with no rhyme nor reason. Here she was holding a child she had not planned and yet life went on with the gathering of corn as it always did. There had to be some purpose to it, some reason for the suffering that came along with the joy. But what, she had no idea.

NOMBULANI

Nombulani's time in seclusion had come to an end. She emerged from the hut looking radiant, with her bright, shining eyes, her smooth dark skin, and her body plump from the sedentary month. She was happy with her new roundness, knowing it would make her even more desirable. The coming of age ceremony for Nombulani began when her family slaughtered the ox. Her father skinned the beast and carved up portions of flesh to be cooked over the fire. On behalf of all the Ancestors, her mother then covered Nombulani's head with mounds of oxfat, to seal their pledge to protect her new life as a woman. Well-wishers from her village and villages nearby had gathered in the circle.

Nombulani began to dance, whirling and stomping her feet, her ceremonial spear clutched tight in her left hand. She danced with joy and thanks and excitement. At such a ceremony it was not uncommon for a girl who was now a woman to make it known which one of the young men she favoured. Today would be the day she would make her choice known. Gathering her courage, uncertain of the outcome, she plunged her spear into the ground at Mandla's feet and danced away around the big circle of family, friends, and villagers. She went from one to another twirling and sweating.

Mandla stared at the spear as its shaft wobbled in the dirt in front of him. He dared not look up. He didn't want anyone to see the conflict in his eyes. Two full rounds of seasons had passed since Ntombi had given birth. His heart still ached for her and yet he knew that to not marry and continue his bloodline would bring his family dishonour.

He looked up to see the freedom on Nombulani's body as it swept around the circle. As she neared him again he gathered his courage, jumped up and began a wild and frenzied dance in front of her. He danced his sorrow, he danced his fear, he danced his surrender to tradition.

Nombulani laughed her joy at his acceptance, and they danced and laughed together while the crowd sang and the women raised their voices in high-pitched ululation.

Ntombi watched as her beloved circled Nombulani's dancing form. She had hoped to throw her spear at Mandla's feet at her own celebration, the one she never had. She had known this day would come, when another would choose Mandla. She had even prayed for it in the hopes that it might release the clutching around her heart whenever she saw him. But now that it was here, the full realization of how alone she was ripped apart all control that she had placed on her loneliness. She slipped away from the circle and returned home through the dark, not able to witness any more of Nombulani's joy.

A few days later Phumzile, Cebesile and Thandhi approached Ntombi at her hut.

"We have come to ask if you would join us in building the wedding hut for Nombulani."

Ntombi braced herself. They did not detect the part of her heart that shriveled at the request, for, of course, they could not have known of her secret betrothal to Mandla. They did not know the longing of her soul that could now never be fulfilled. Hlwelo had destroyed any possibility for a future with her beloved. To prepare the hut where he and Nombulani would lay was the cruelest punishment the Gods could decree.

"I am humbled by your request and I would be happy to work alongside you," Ntombi said.

And truly, part of her was sincere. To be invited meant she was no longer an outcast, she had been fully accepted once again as a valued member of the village.

The four women set out into the veld, each carrying a large woven basket, their mission to find anthills. Off to the east they traveled until they found a collection of them, the reddish brown mounds rising to various heights. They set about collecting the earth filled with the larvae the ants had deposited. Dispersed through the soil were the bodies of dead ants. Their last secreted saliva created a granular texture that was ideal for the surface of the floor of the new hut.

With full baskets, they returned to the cleared site in the village that was to be the beginning of the new life for Mandla and Nombulani. This site would house their love mat, their lovemaking, their babies. Ntombi imagined Mandla's strong body knowing she could never touch it again, never feel the thrill of seeing his excitement as it rose proud and sure. The memory of him singed her body: the way he would feel his way over her skin like a blind man seeking out all there was to be known, the way their bodies fit in such perfect symmetry, the way the juices of their mouths tasted together. She would never feel him again.

She shook her head to dislodge the images. She returned her focus to combining the ant earth with water to make a thick paste. They spread it on the ground to create the floor of the hut, leaving it to bake in the sun. It would dry to a finish harder than stone. The final step was to scrub it with cow manure and then polish it with large pebbles for a smooth and shiny surface. The women set off once more to gather saplings, which they then intricately lashed together to make the walls of the hut.

The grandmothers sat together in the centre of the village making the thatching for the roof from the grasses the younger women had brought to them.

In the evening around the fire, the women bit off pieces of ostrich eggshell and then ground them on stone to round the edges. In the morning the pile of these unique disks were handed to Mandla's male friends who pierced the centres with deadly sharp spearheads. The women then threaded them one by one along dried cow sinews and a heavy, ghostly necklace was ready for the bride to wear at her wedding.

All the women gathered together – friends, grandmothers, and sisters – to present Nombulani with the necklace. Overjoyed to receive it, she went from one woman to the next touching her forehead to theirs in acknowledgment and thanks. They shared a simple meal and chatted over the details of the upcoming wedding.

After the meal, Ntombi congratulated Nombulani once again and returned to her hut. She lay down. Softly she pressed her back into the mat imagining it to be Mandla's back. What would it feel like to touch their warmth, spine to spine? She thought of how soon he would lay with Nombulani. How could she have turned him away knowing he would eventually choose another? But there had been no other way. Their love for one another could never have erased the shame she would have brought on him. And so she lay there loving him in her mind. Her body warmed with the image of the contour of his forearm, the strength that lay beneath the rounded muscle, the sleek line that led down his arm to thick fingers, fingers that had softly stroked her face, hands that had held her firmly as his mouth reached for hers. She felt his lingering breath still upon her lips after all this time. She must stop this. She must let go of him. It was torture for her and unfair to him, for she knew that he felt her body call for him in these moments. She knew she held him captive, not allowing him to fully give himself to Nombulani. She had to release him. Her body coiled into a ball. She rocked back and forth eventually coming to stillness on her side, her tears spilling onto the vacant space beside her on the mat.

WEDDING

Walking a step behind her father with eyes lowered, Nombulani watched the dust puff into the air as her feet swept over the earth. She marveled that her father, a great hunter, so swift and accurate in a kill, was also such a gentle man. She thought of Mandla and recognized how like her father he was.

Nombulani and Bongani walked through the village to the gate of the isibaya. As they entered the enclosure, Nombulani felt the presence of all the young women who had previously entered the heart of the village with their fathers on the day before their wedding. She savoured every moment of this last opportunity to be alone with her father.

Bongani pulled Nombulani's head toward him and kissed the top of her tight curls. Then looking directly into the eyes of his favourite child he said, "You have grown into a fine young woman. Tomorrow you will belong to another man. I will no longer be the one to protect you. It is time."

The cows turned lazily to acknowledge their presence, their tails flicking back and forth, their long eyelashes fluttering as flies landed and buzzed about. There were many cattle now, nine more having been recently added from Mandla's family, the agreed-upon *libola* price. She was pleased that she had been considered worthy of a good price that showed how much Mandla valued her as his soon-to-be wife. It revealed the respect he felt for how well she had been raised. Nombulani went from one cow to the next stroking the warm skin of their necks. She saved for last, Kalazone, her favourite. Many times she had pressed her shoulder into these flanks as she squatted beside her, squirting fresh milk into a wooden pail. Her mouth became moist with the memory of its sweet, warm taste.

She looked into the soft eyes of this gentle beast.

"You be good, now, don't you go kicking over the pot of milk when Nomusa comes to take my place." Her hand glided over the mosaic of Kalazone's red and white hide. She whispered into her ear, "I hope your name will prove true, and that these tears I cry from sorrow now at leaving you and my family will turn to tears of joy in my new life."

She walked to the Buffalo Thorn tree.

"*Igugu thandiwe*, Ancestors. My thanks for the protection you have given me. I have come to say goodbye, I must now go to the homestead of Mandla's Ancestors. But I ask you to remain with me as I become his wife. Ubaba and Umama have promised me they will continue to let you know where I am and what is happening in my life. I ask you to protect me wherever I may be."

She pressed her forehead against the rough bark and closed her eyes.

Bongani smiled at his daughter.

"May your husband be skilled in the hunts and may you bear him many male children."

Together they left the isibaya and returned to their huts.

The next morning Nombulani woke early with a prickly feeling on her scalp. The excitement of the impending day was jumping in and out of her head and all through her body. She opened her eyes to see her mother already stooped over the black pot, stirring the mealie meal. She watched the smoke from the fire as it wound its way around the centre post of the hut. It snaked its way up and through the hanging baskets of maize, ensuring the death of any termites that might still be lurking.

She thought about all the little deaths that happen all the time. They are all around us, she thought, and we don't even notice... the ants we squish under our mats as we lay down to sleep, that our feet crunch as we walk everywhere, that our brooms catapult as we sweep, that the plough destroys as it furrows the red earth to make way for the potential of more life, the ending of my life here to begin my new life with Mandla.

"Umama, I will miss you," she said, aloud.

Her mother stopped mid-stir and slowly straightened her body. She, too, was feeling the weight of this day. All the preparation, all the excitement, had seemed endless and yet, here they were, the day her daughter would leave her side had arrived...too soon.

"Mandla is a good man," she said and she meant it.

It was the one reassuring thing in the face of the huge vacuum that loomed with her daughter's imminent departure. There should have been other children clambering about for her to scold for making her life a misery, but they were dead. All of them, except Nombulani, dead.

Ever since the Great Fire, she had not dared to allow her heart to open for fear that what was left of it would shatter into an irreparable heap of shards. Afraid that if she gathered her remaining child in her arms she would vanish in a whisper of smoke. She couldn't look at her daughter, couldn't tell her how her heart was breaking. She had to be strong and smile when the time came for Nombulani to walk away from her for the last time, without a backward glance.

"Come, Nombulani, enough with lying around as if today were just another day. There is much to do. There is a long walk ahead. Get up!"

Nombulani sat up, the sting of her mother's words still landing. Today she had hoped for a loving connection with her mother, possibly the last chance to see something in her eyes or hear something in her voice to reassure her that the bond between mother and daughter, even if not demonstrated, was strong and unbreakable. Today she needed to know that the life ahead of her was still deeply rooted in the life she was leaving behind.

"You're right," she said, with an edge of anger that always rose to cover her hurt.

All of Nombulani's women relatives gathered in her grandmother's hut. After a week of preparations, nights around the fire talking of things she must know to be a good wife, sharing stories of their own weddings and lives with their husbands, the time had come for Nombulani to collect her wedding adornments and leave her mother behind. Her relatives gathered the blankets, brightly decorated mats, clay pots, brooms, beads, baskets, drums, necklaces, and skins; all gifts for Mandla's relatives. They stepped outside, ready for the long walk to Mandla's family homestead at the far end of the village, up the hillside.

Nombulani's mother handed her the ceremonial shield made especially by Bongani for this wedding day walk.

"This is for your protection," she said, "to keep you safe on your journey to your new home. And this knife," she aggressively slashed the air too close to Nombulani's face, "the ties are now severed between you and your family," she said, her voice steady.

She took the long stick covered at the end with resin from the *Msulusulu* tree, poked it into the fire until it caught alight. Handing it to her daughter she said, "And this is to light the path so that you don't lose your way. And here is your veil. Make sure you do not look directly at Mandla or things will not go well for you in your new life."

She wanted so much to hold Nombulani, hold her fast and never let her go. Instead she said, "Hambagashla, my daughter, go well."

As was the custom, Nombulani's mother would not be attending the wedding. This would be their last time together with Nombulani as a single woman, the last time she would be under her mother's care. Nombulani looked into her mother's hard eyes. It had been too much to expect any tenderness; even so, she felt the pain from the lack of it.

The other women were bustling about hoisting their bundles atop their heads, all chatter and excitement. Grandmother, sister, aunts, cousins waited while Nombulani left the hut and squeezed through the opening at the top of the isibaya. She passed by the Buffalo Thorn tree bowing her head to the Ancestors. She passed by the cattle, her fingers reaching out to brush against the warm hides. She went out the bottom of the isibaya. She wondered if her mother was watching her or whether she had already gone back into the hut. She resisted the impulse to defy custom, to turn and look behind her, to check one last time to see if there was any comfort to be found there. But, not wishing to bring bad luck upon her marriage, and, more strongly, not wanting to carry more heartbreak, she kept her eyes focused straight in front of her as she walked toward her future.

The women walked on, the flames from their flickering sticks casting light and shadows. The sun was still low in the sky. As they approached Mandla's homestead they began to sing a hearty, full-throated tune, the aunt singing out the lead, the others echoing the phrase in glorious harmonies, ululations ringing the announcement of their arrival.

Mandla's family pretended not to see Nombulani as she entered the cooking hut and took her place with the women of his family; one of the lighthearted traditions surrounding her wedding. When she emerged her relatives brought forward the cow they had brought with them and Mandla's family brought their cow forward. The two together were sacrificed to the Ancestors, asking them to bless this union of families. The men set about skinning and carving the animals and the women then prepared the meat for cooking. Some of the women stayed by the fire placing the pieces of meat on skewers lining them up on racks above the fire as flashes of flame licked up pieces of dripping fat. The smell of the burning meat filled the homestead. Gourds were filled with sorghum beer.

Plenty of meat, corn, yams, melons and drink were ready for the festivities that would begin after the wedding ceremony.

It was time for Nombulani to prepare. Her relatives fussed about her, tying small skin sacks filled with pebbles around her ankles, fastening the leather skirt around her waist, putting over her shoulders the beaded covering that fell low enough to cover her breasts. Around her neck they tied a necklace, made from the hair of the goat her father had sacrificed to the Ancestors, announcing her betrothal to Mandla.

Alongside the necklace she wore a duplicate of the beaded love-note she had given to Mandla when he had accepted her as his intended. Around her waist hung her knife with the blade pointed down to assure the groom's family of her virginity. And last, the beaded veil was placed on her head. The colourful strands of beads, hanging in front of her eyes, swayed whenever she moved her head. There was much chatter and excitement.

Mandla's brothers and uncles, father and friends happily placed the leather skin around his waist, long enough to cover his buttocks in back, and to cover his groin in front. They tied strips of animal skins slaughtered in this betrothal time around his ankles and wrists. They placed the leopard skin over his shoulders and the braided leopard skin ring upon his head. He wore the beaded necklace Nombulani had made for him. He tried to not think of the one Ntombi had given him at the river. The one no one knew about. The one he kept hidden in a sack in his hut.

At last Nombulani and Mandla came together in the centre of the village, each escorted by their entourage and accompanied by singing and laughter. Nombulani kept her head down, eyes lowered. The Chief solemnly began to recite the words to join them together. She shyly glanced sideways to take the smallest peek at her betrothed and unexpectedly looked directly into Mandla's eyes. Nombulani's breath caught in her throat and she quickly turned her eyes down, her heart pounding.

Just at that moment Mandla had turned to look at the veiled bride, trying to reassure himself that all would be well in spite of the clutching around his heart.

The Chief concluded his words, and the dancing began. Nombulani lined up with her women relatives and friends. Together they started, their feet in rhythm, the pebbles in the sacks at Nombulani's ankles ringing out a percussive sound. They advanced toward the line of men seated on the ground in front of them, Mandla in the middle, his spear and shield in hand. Nombulani was not so sure of herself now. Her steps were not as carefree as she had anticipated them to be for this dance of wife to husband. She smiled in spite of it and tried to relax into the rhythm and told herself she was being too superstitious, that the beginning of her new life with Mandla would be everything she had hoped for.

The dancing and feasting lasted long into the night. When everyone was spent, Nombulani cleaned and swept as the newly married woman would do, to prove to her new family that she was capable and able to care well for her new husband.

Exhausted but excited Nombulani finally entered the hut and lay down on their wedding mat. She covered herself with the thick skin blanket, a present from her mother-in- law, and shivered even in the presence of the warmth it offered.

Mandla sat down on the edge of the mat and stared at the polished floor of their new home. After a few moments of silence he turned to Nombulani, reached out his hand and slowly lowered the blanket exposing her nakedness. He ran his fingers over her breastbone and encircled each of her breasts feeling her nipples harden in response to his touch. He took his hand away and stared again at the floor. He looked at Nombulani, lay down beside her and gathered her in his arms.

Mandla knew that what he must do now was to let go. Ntombi was no longer within his possibility. He was here now beside another woman, his wife. Ntombi will never lie beside him as his wife. He must let go. He hears the soft expectant breath of Nombulani beside him. He knows she is waiting. Waiting for him to fulfill his duty on this, their wedding night. He would not be seen as a man unless he takes her. But how can he...his body is numb, no, not numb, not numb at all. It is on fire with sorrow, with doubt, with longing, but not longing for Nombulani... rather a longing for the life he had envisioned, for the joy that had been taken from him, for the touch of Ntombi's skin on his. His body was fired with rage, with a desperate desire for revenge. He should scour the ends of the earth to find Hlwelo and kill him, no, not kill him, but to slowly and cruelly torture him for taking his beautiful woman to beyond his having. He heard Nombulani's breathing change, felt her hand tentative on his skin.

"What is it, Mandla," she whispered. "Have I displeased you?"

What could he say? He had no words. His throat was dry, his heartbeat painful. He waited. He must say something. "I'm sorry," he said. "I am going to need some time."

And with that he covered her with the blanket, and got up. He took a mat from its basket hanging on the wall, unfurled it and lay down, his back to Nombulani, the mud wall bleary in front of his eyes. After a few moments he rose and left the hut.

Nombulani took the emptiness beside her into her body and felt its sharp edge. The air was cold against her skin where a moment before the promise of his body pressed warm against her limbs. What had made him rise from the mat and leave her with only the night pressing in?

The time leading up to the wedding celebration had carried her feet above the ground, her heart larger in her chest. And now something felt very wrong. She was afraid. She rose from the mat and, as she left the hut, saw his silhouette by the isibaya. She went to him and bowing her head asked, "What is it, Mandla?"

The wind whispered through the leaves of the Buffalo Thorn tree. The cattle shifted and snorted.

"I fear I have betrayed you before I knew you," he said.

The air became still. The darkness spread below her feet. She waited, not knowing if the earth would swallow her. She waited not knowing if his voice would rescue her. The wind rose again.

Mandla spoke, his voice slow and thick. "I'm sorry. I cannot love you as you wish. I cannot love you as I had wished. I thought I was in command of my heart but it is not so."

He turned to face her and felt across the darkness and took her hand. "I promise you I will try to bend my heart toward you. I will return when I know it can be done."

Nombulani felt the warmth of his hand evaporate as he let go. She watched his shadow dissolve into the night. The darkness at her feet widened and she fell in.

Mandla made his way to the river. His feet knew every step of the way. Countless times he had trod that path, sometimes with his feet actually touching the dirt, sometimes just with his mind reliving the memory of coming to the river to find her, then seeing her… her form, and her spirit that moved about her shoulders. Once or twice he had seen a glow behind her that he could only believe was the Ancestors hovering over her. And then, there was the music of her body. As it resounded with effortless beauty, his own body would enter a state of exquisite suspension.

He knelt by the river, the moon a ghost in the sky, and he prayed. His closed his eyes. His belly rose with the intake of damp air. He bowed his head as he exhaled his confusion into the night.

"Help me," he cried. "I have taken another woman to be mine when my heart is not free. I betray my love by taking my wife. I betray my wife by loving my love. I have tried to believe it does not matter, but the lack of power in my manhood shows me the truth. I have failed. I am worthless to both women. Help me to know the way."

Mandla waited, hoping to hear the voices of the Ancestors speak to him as he knew they spoke to Ntombi. He opened his eyes. The moon grew larger in the sky. It moved toward him and hovered just over the surface of the river, its light intensifying, vibrating through his bones. He shuddered in pain. His body crumpled on the sand and he wept. He wept for his lost love. He wept for his waiting wife.

Ntombi could not sleep. She lay on her mat with no comfortable place to be. A strange sensation prickled the length of her legs. No amount of changing position would put an end to it. She turned toward Doyenne, hearing her soft breath moving in and out of her body. Gogo's breath from across the hut was thick and heavy.

Quietly, Ntombi rose from her mat and walked out of the hut. Her legs carried her past the isibaya, out the gate and down to the river. The moon hung low and strange. She stopped, taking in its unnatural glow. A stream of light shot from its centre and landed on the opposite bank. There, on the sand, was a black heap moving in a jagged rhythm. She heard a moan.

Her feet stepped into the river, a slight chill rushing through her body. She waded through the water. It rose to the tops of her thighs. As she emerged on the other side, the water dripped down her legs. The moon's light began to vibrate as she approached the dark shape. She knew it was Mandla. She knew her legs had carried her here to find him. She saw his face, moist and miserable, lift from the sand, his beautiful face distorted and drawn. She saw the flicker of recognition in his eyes. She knelt beside him and gently lifting his head, cradled it in her lap and stroked his forehead. She felt his chest rise and fall with each sob, her own face also awash with tears.

"I have betrayed you by marrying another," Mandla cried. "I thought I was free but you are in command of my heart. I will leave Nombulani tonight forever and come to you. Bongani can keep the cattle. It is a small price to pay to have my heart whole again. Please let me come and claim you as I should have done. I don't care that you have been damaged. I will look after Doyenne. You will both have my love and protection. Please let me come to you."

Ntombi waited, the struggle between submission and restraint fierce within her breast.

"It is my fault," she said. "I have been unfair to you and Nombulani. I have kept your heart inside of mine. I feared I would not be strong enough if I let it go. But I know now that the Ancestors are keeping me safe. I have Doyenne to care for and Gogo to guide me. I have strong reasons to stay on the earth and I no longer fear that my life is in danger. It is time for me to let you go. I will go to my Grandmother's hut and burn the white heather. I will ask the Ancestors for the strength to let my spirit release you," and, in a voice she could barely find, added, "and I pray that your full manhood will rise and claim Nombulani as your wife. I will pray for your happiness."

Mandla's body sagged knowing that no words would sway her now. He knew, too, that it was as hard for her to speak these words as it was for him to hear them. She loved him. He never doubted that. He kept his head in her lap for a very long time knowing it would be the last time.

Slowly he stood and, with a gentle hand, pulled her to standing. He lifted her hand to his mouth and pressed his full lips against her black skin.

"I will take my strength from your strength," he said softly, letting go of her hand.

He turned and walked into the shadows, the moon dimming and receding high into the sky.

Mandla walked back to his village, entered his homestead, walked past the isibaya and into his hut. He lay down on the wedding mat beside Nombulani.

"I am here," he said. "I have come back to you. I will take you fully and properly as my wife. But it will not be tonight."

And with those words he rolled onto his back and stared into the dark.

The first time Mandla made love with Nombulani, it was tentative. In the dim light of the hut he was glad she could not see his eyes, for they kept drifting away from the face beneath him. His gaze constantly turned to the side, past Nombulani's shoulder, past the packed earth of the floor, past the confines of the hut. His manhood was strong and hard but there was no change in his breath, no sharp intake with each stroke, no moan of pleasure. There was, in the end, no release, just a quiet withdrawal. He did put his arms around Nombulani wanting so much for her to not feel the lack of his presence of heart. He cradled her small shoulders in his strong embrace but his pelvis backed away, leaving a space between them. His toes curled in on themselves. He would not slip into sleep with his body content and spent as he had imagined the nights in marriage would end. But then there was nothing about this he had imagined. All of this now had to be made up moment to moment, in the absence of love.

Nombulani was relieved to finally go freely out into the village now that their marriage had been consummated. Now she could finally turn the knife at her belt up to signify she had been fully taken as his wife. How could she have gone out into the village for all to see that he had not lain with her? How could she have borne the shame, the looks that surely would have greeted her? She had hoped his reticence was shyness, but she knew now there was something else. But, at least she could finally walk among his family and in the village with her head held high and with a smile on her lips that belied the dread in her heart.

Nombulani watched as Mandla walked through their homestead. He went to the isibaya to check the cattle. The musty smell of animal dung and sweat reached her, even at this distance. The coloured patterns on their hides were stark in the fading light. She watched Mandla's broad hands running over a cow's flank. She imagined the feel of the warm breathing skin as it rose and fell. She knew that the unreachable place in Mandla was not just his quiet nature or the seriousness with which he approached their marriage. It wasn't something she had or had not done. It was something else.

The sun flashed through the lidloti tree landing on Mandla's face. He looked blank, as he often did. What was in his heart, she longed to know. The cattle snorted and shifted. Mandla left the isibaya and walked out of the homestead. Nombulani followed him, careful to not be seen, as he continued far through the village. She wasn't spying on him exactly, she told herself, but she was following him. She wanted to observe every turn of his head, every dusty footstep. At last he stopped and somewhat shrank in stature, as if wanting to hide himself. She followed his gaze. It landed on the hut where Ntombi lived with her bastard child and her grandmother.

Nombulani's eyes darted back to Mandla and there it was. All the pain that he would never let her see, all the anguish that lay in the dark between them on their sleeping mat, all the love that was never in his touch on her skin. Nombulani's chest recoiled as if the force of an angry fist had fired its way through her skin, cracking open her ribs. She gasped for air. There it was – what she really had not wanted to know but could not stop herself from finding out. How much easier to think she herself had been lacking, for at least then she could have done something, changed herself in some way to appear more pleasing. But from this there was no rescue, there was no remedy, no possibility of standing in front of Mandla and have him see only her. She would be forever seen through the mirage of Ntombi.

Nombulani turned away and returned to their hut and waited for his return. Nombulani watched Mandla's body as he entered the hut. She saw his chest deflate slightly, even as he said, "Yebo, Nombulani." She saw the effort it took for him to smile.

Setting aside the fear in her heart, she said, "Mandla, I wish to speak with you." She saw his right eye twitch.

"Please come and sit with me."

Mandla looked at the ground and then moved to the stump beside the small smouldering fire.

"I have been following you. I needed to know what it was that has kept you from me. And now I understand. I saw on your face the longing and pain as you looked at Ntombi's hut. It is her that you love. It is to her that you have pledged yourself, not to me. I see there is no room for me. If I could, I would return to my father's care, but I could not bear the shame. So I will wait in your care until a moment comes when you might open a piece of your heart to me. I will not ask for much. I will ask for patience so that I may not become bitter. I trust that my happiness lies with you. If I did not believe so I would not have married you. But then, I did not realize your heart was not free. I will ask the spirits of our Ancestors to intervene on my behalf and if my request is unsuccessful

I will ask the Chief to honourably release me from my pledge to you."

Mandla nodded his head.

"Yes," he said. "It is true." He waited, not sure he was capable of what he was about to say. "And I promise you I will stop my thoughts of her. I have pledged myself to you as you have to me, and I will honour that pledge. I will also ask the Ancestors for strength. You are a good woman."

Early the next morning, after no sleep, Mandla rose quietly. He heard the small sound of Nombulani's breath. He knew she had not slept much throughout the night either. When the depth of her breath meant she had finally drifted into sleep, he took this moment to go to the sack hanging on the wall of his hut. He lifted it off its hook and went out of the hut to the isibaya. The morning light was but a whisper in the sky. In the dim light he began to dig close to the Buffalo Thorn tree. When the hole was deep enough, he opened the bag and held the beaded love necklace Ntombi had given him. He looked at the colours, faint in the low light, remembering how she had told him what each colour meant. He pressed it to his forehead, he pressed it to his heart, he pressed it to his lips. He put it back in the sack and buried it in the ground, vowing to bury with it his longing for Ntombi.

TIME PASSING

Doyenne had grown strong over the last four full rounds of seasons. She was an adventurous young thing and Ntombi was often looking up from the washing to make sure she hadn't gotten up to some mischief. Doyenne was sitting on a branch that had lodged itself at the side of the river. She had crawled along its length to sit on the end that protruded out over the flowing water. Held tight in her hand was a thick piece of corn bread left over from yesterday's meal.

Ntombi was close by, kneading the wet clothes in a rocking motion rolling them over the rocks, coaxing the dust and sweat from them. She turned to check on Doyenne. The little girl was nibbling on the dry corn bread, swinging her legs back and forth in the space between her seat and the water. She was humming to herself. She had such a sweet nature and, despite the lightness of her skin, was a beautiful child. No one could deny it, and, thankfully, most seemed not to care anymore about the difference that separated her from the rest of the tribe. Doyenne smiled at her mother and waved with the crumbling piece of bread. A flash of yellow appeared. A weaverbird seized this exact moment to dart from the riverbank reeds and swoop over Doyenne's outstretched hand and grab at the chunk of bread. Doyenne's body jerked in surprise and then she giggled, a high trickle of sound, her other hand raised to her mouth in sheer delight.

Ntombi laughed at the bemused gleam in Doyenne's eyes and felt a great relief that the impertinent bird had not unseated her daughter. In spite of her harsh beginnings, Doyenne had become her life and her joy. She watched as Doyenne inched her way off the branch and, once back on the riverbank, began her favourite game of finding the biggest rocks her little hands could lift and throwing them as far as she could into the laughing river. With each splash Doyenne shrieked with joy. Ntombi looked away and continued pounding the dust and dirt from the clothes. Then the world became too still, too silent. Ntombi's body froze. Her head jerked up. Where was Doyenne? Where was the laughter that should have followed the splash? The horrid splash that had happened too far down the river, the horrid splash that Ntombi had misinterpreted as Doyenne's game. A current surged through her body. She sprang up, propelled forward, thrashing through the river, its water spraying up onto the quiet rocks. She pressed forward through the resistance of the water, heart choking in her throat until she reached her child. Doyenne's body was swaying in the current, moving one way then pulled gently back by the insistent reeds ensnaring her, her eyes wide with surprise, her red blood diluting to clear on its way to the sea. Ntombi frantically grabbed Doyenne into her arms. She squeezed and squeezed trying to force the river's poison out of the limp body, until there was nothing left to do but hold her close against her breast. She rocked back and forth, back and forth, wails of anguish slicing the air, until she too became as still as her child.

Gogo abruptly stopped her beadwork. The light was lowering in the sky. It had been too long since Ntombi had left with Doyenne. She staggered to her feet and went to find Gosololo.

"Help me," she said, "I have to find Ntombi and Doyenne. My body tells me something is wrong and I must find them. I am filled with fear."

"Where do you think they might be?" Gosololo asked.

"At the beginning of the day Ntombi went to the river to do the washing."

Gosololo took her friend by the arm and together they rushed down the path to the river. The day was still, too still. The air pressed against them, hard and suffocating. They walked through the trail in the reeds and came to the riverbank. They saw the washing abandoned, a piece of clothing dislodged and floated downstream. Their eyes followed its path and as it passed under the tree branch that leaned far out over the river they saw the heap of bodies slumped together at the edge of the water. The two women ran, their feet slipping and stumbling over the rocks. They arrived at the side of Ntombi and saw the dull green eyes of Doyenne staring into nothingness, the gash on the side of her head raw and gaping. Ntombi was still, too still, she didn't move. She just looked into the river. Even when the women touched her arm and stroked her forehead still she did not move. Gosololo lifted Doyenne's lifeless body out of Ntombi's arms as Gogo lifted Ntombi to standing. They made their way back to the village and laid the silent Ntombi on her mat in the hut. They wrapped Doyenne in her goatskin, her face uncovered. Gogo lit some white heather and called on the Ancestors to receive the spirit of Doyenne. Gogo knew this pain, knew the delicate thread that now held Ntombi. She prayed for strength to help her granddaughter survive and find her way. Why had the gods visited such anguish on them?

Why was there so much suffering? There was too much loss, too much sorrow. She did not understand the darkness in life.

The village came together to mourn the loss of Doyenne and to offer prayers for her to be received by the Ancestors. They also prayed for the healing of Ntombi's spirit. Mandla stayed at the edge of the gathering not wishing to see the pain on Ntombi's face, not wishing to add in any way to her torment.

Ntombi went through her days quietly, attending as best she could to daily chores but her heart was clouded and dull. At night, in fits of sleep and wakefulness, her mind was like a ribbon of fire. Her tongue curled up to press on the roof of her mouth in an attempt to steady herself. All she wanted was to sleep, to drift into the spongy bed of unconsciousness. Her fingers would tremble. She would hear the splash and swallow hard. She opened her eyes, but all she could see was the sharp rock, the tangle of reeds wound around the feet of her discoloured girl, holding her fast, submerged. Would she ever be free of this nightmare? Would she ever hear anything other than this death drum sounding in her ears? It was only a split second, Ntombi thought. How could such a thing happen in a split second? Overpowering guilt gnawed though her heart and her belly. Every time the memory exploded, her stomach clenched and convulsed in waves of nausea. Her mind reeled, the image of the lifeblood draining from her sweet child repeated itself in an endless punishing loop. She relived this scene over and over, never able to find a different ending, never able to forgive herself.

One morning, Ntombi went to the river to collect water. She put the pot into the flowing river, the same river that had once held such joy for her. She felt the pull of its current as it filled the vessel. When it was full she placed the woven reed ring on her head, and nestled the pot in it and began her way back to the village. She was tired and the sun was hot. She sat down on the cracked, orange earth. She still had far to go but it didn't seem as if there was any rush. As she sat, she watched a dung beetle stagger across the path. Amazing creatures, these, able to carry such a huge burden so many, many times their own body weight. She often wondered how much she was capable of carrying. Oh, she knew her arms and legs were strong. She could carry the earthen jug of water balanced on her head weighted down by the precious water from the river. At the same time she had been able to carry her baby close in the faded piece of cloth, as well as sticks for the fire bundled together on her back. But she didn't think her spirit was strong enough to carry the weight of Doyenne's death. It was too heavy. She had no spark left, no desire to live. Her days were dark and painful. Was it possible she had ever felt joy? It all seemed such a far off memory, irretrievable, no longer possible. She often looked around her and wondered why people kept on living, how they could smile and keep going. It all seemed so futile – to get up each day, do the same chores, go to bed at night only to get up the next day and do them all again – for what? She often thought of the great relief it would be to jump into oblivion, to end this endless pain.

Ntombi wondered, what is beyond this dusty path? What is beyond the river? What is beyond this life? What if she just continued to walk and never turned back? What if she did end it? She looked up at the sky, the unrelenting brightness, the intensity that seemed to dare her to keep thinking these dangerous thoughts, taunting her. I will end it, she decided, a wave of relief spreading over her. Should she plan her exit or just let some trance overtake her that would lead her to that fate? She got up off the ground, ready now to resume her walk with the water jug balanced on her head, to return to the village as she did every day, to go about her business and no one would know that anything was different. But she would know. She could already feel the difference in her walk. She would have to be careful. She would have to keep her eyes lowered or someone might notice the change. Gosololo would notice. She always did. She knew everything. She could tell you were going to have a baby before you knew it. Sometimes it seemed that Gogo knew her better than she knew herself. She would have to be careful.

As her steps took her back to her village, her mind let go and seemed to float and hover somewhere above her, moving further and further into a state of nothing. Everything merged into one, the heat, the dust, the weight of the water and the jug. She could see the haze of the heat undulating in front of her and she entered into its waves. It seemed as though she was moving in slow motion, or not moving at all. It was a caressing feeling. It was like a cool drink of water when one is thirsty. There was no need to hurry. It was all being taken care of and she allowed herself to surrender in that suspended place.

As she approached the village she slowly came back to an awareness of her surroundings as the sounds of the children tapping their sticks in the dirt playing their games entered her consciousness. She felt the heaviness of the jug, where before it had been weightless. What had just happened? She had gone somewhere, but where? She felt different. Something inside the pain had shifted. She removed the jug from off her head, placed it and the braided ring on the ground outside the hut and went inside to check on Gogo.

There in the corner, lying on the well-worn mat was her beloved grandmother. She lay there quiet and still, her breath barely audible. She was old and tired. It was clear she did not have long to live. She had been slowing down for years, but about a month ago an uneasy feeling began in her belly. At first they thought she had eaten too many of the berries that made her stomach cramp but this had lasted too long and, if anything, was getting worse. If it had been the berries it would have passed through her and left her weak but pain free. This pain was increasing and with the pain came the recognition that the end of her time was drawing near.

For Ntombi to watch her grandmother fading away was like seeing another piece of herself dying. It was as if they were part of the same soul. She saw her grandmother stir and motion her to come closer. Ntombi knelt down beside her and leaned in close to her grandmother's beautifully wrinkled face.

"Where have you been, my sweet girl?" she asked.

"I have been to the river to fetch the water for the mid-day meal. I am sorry I was gone so long."

Gogo paused. She knew well the fragile state her granddaughter was in. She knew in her own bones the struggle to stay alive in the face of devastation. When she lost Lindiwe and the others it was unbearable. She owed her life to Ntombi. She had known that she must survive to care for her and watch her grow into a woman. Ntombi had been her one light in the expanse of darkness. But all Ntombi had was her, an old woman close to death. She knew her time was near and she feared for Ntombi's life.

"Your voice has changed. What happened out in the veld?"

Ntombi thought, how was it that this woman, so ready to join the Ancestors, could still read her? It was as if Gogo had been with her on the road, inside her head and heart. Ntombi's body tightened at the thought of losing this beautiful being who had raised her, cared for her and known her so deeply. Her grandmother had been her source of strength, had been the one who never thought of her or Doyenne as a mistake, who protected her and taught her the ways of wisdom, knowledge, and heart. She would not harm herself while Gogo was still alive. She would wait. But after Gogo was gone there would be no way she could continue without her guidance and counsel. Ntombi looked around Gogo's humble hut and marveled at how all her life history was reflected everywhere she looked.

After a long pause she said, "I am not sure what happened, it was a strange experience…like being there but not being there at the same time. I don't understand it. Something happened when I looked into the heat waves. My heart that had been so heavy seemed to lift for a moment."

Gogo smiled. "You entered into the space between the heat and the air, through the haze of this world into the other world…the Ancestors opened a window for your heart. They have always been with you. After the Great Fire they brought you back to us. I will die soon and they will call you. You will know when."

Ntombi was unable to speak. She worried over her grandmother's words… they will call you… she didn't want to be called … she wanted to die, to join her Grandmother with the Ancestors.

Gogo smiled and put her weathered hand on top of Ntombi's smooth skin. Her touch was cool and soothing.

"When I saw you walking toward us at the river after the Great Fire it was like watching you return from the dead. You had come back to me, my most precious one. Everything around you dissolved. You began to glow with a radiant light that I had only known before in the dreamtime. I ran towards you and when I held you I felt my body and yours melt into each other. I heard a rushing sound in my ears and then the singing of the Ancestors, their voices strong in harmony and power and indescribable joy. When the world reformed and you were you, and I was me, my heart knew you had been touched by the call of the Ancestors. One day you would have to leave me and walk through the land on a solitary, dangerous journey. My heart saw that you had the power to walk through the crack in the earth and return again with much insight, knowledge and wisdom. You, my most loved one, would follow in the footsteps of your great grandmother and become a powerful Sangoma, a great blessing to the people and the land. All your pain would be transformed into *muti*, powerful medicine to help others heal their pain. It is a deep gift that is born of deep sorrow. I have always wondered when the day would come that you would go. Now I see that the Ancestors have smiled on me and will not come to call you until I can be one of them. I will witness and help you make this transition from dutiful granddaughter to powerful seer. My heart is smiling. I am at peace now knowing this."

Ntombi felt a stab of guilt, knowing her resolve was not what Gogo would want. She saw Gogo shift her body slightly but it was a signal that Ntombi knew well. It meant Gogo knew something was bothering her and was completely ready to hear whatever she had to say. Ntombi looked into her grandmother's eyes.

"I am sorry, Grandmother," she began, "but I don't think that I can follow where the Ancestors may ask me to go. It is too hard a life. It is too much responsibility. I am too broken."

Ntombi looked down feeling her throat tighten as her eyes filled. Gogo waited.

"What if I should interpret the Ancestors incorrectly and cause great harm to someone who seeks me out for relief from their suffering? I could not bear to add to their misery by my incompetence."

"You doubt yourself, my child, and that is a good thing, for those who assume they are always right and will never falter are dangerous. They do not listen well. Those who are mindful of the delicate trust that has been placed in them are more willing to step aside and allow the Ancestors to speak. Your doubt allows you to surrender yourself to the wisdom that will come through you, for you know and trust it is greater than you; part of you, yes, but bigger than your limited mind can access. There is no need to rush. Patience, my girl. When the time comes, you will know your path and how to follow it. It will be clear."

Gogo smiled and put her weathered hand on top of Ntombi's smooth skin. Her touch was cool and soothing. Ntombi did not tell her grandmother of her decision to join her soon with the Ancestors. She felt uneasy but she took some comfort in her grandmother's words.

Ntombi kissed Gogo's weathered cheek.

"I will look in on you again soon. You rest now, Grandmother."

Gogo closed her eyes and slipped into sleep. Ntombi went outside to tend to her chores. She stepped into the hut with the long, low, flat stone where the corn was ground into flour. Where Grandmother's hut had smelled of herbs and decay, this hut smelled of flour and dust. The sides of the hut were solid and sturdy. She had helped to build this hut years ago. It had been a source of pride for her when she was asked to help build it. It was part of now being accepted as a woman in the tribe. She remembered the day long ago when Gogo had taught her to close her eyes, feel the rhythm of her body with each pass of the stone over the dried kernels as it released the powdery flour.

When Ntombi had enough flour for the bread, she put down the stone and left the hut. She walked across the dry, red earth, the heat of the late afternoon hanging lightly around her tired shoulders. Her pace slowed, her breathing deepened. Her sight began to shift. She could feel her eyes start to relax and pull back. Looking down she saw a thin, jagged crack appear in the dust. Gradually, it began to widen and deepen, growing into a large, dark, bottomless pit. A slight wind began to blow, increasing until she felt her body pushing against its force in order to stay on her feet. She could hear roaring in her ears. Out from the pit rose nebulous forms and shapes, dark and misty. They swirled and danced. They hovered about the abyss and began moving towards Ntombi. She tried to calm her rising pulse, willing herself to surrender to the visitation, to allow its message to enter her without obstruction. Why did this come to her? She did not ask for it, she did not want it, yet she knew to disallow it would kill her. And yet, she knew to allow it could also kill her. She could either succumb to her desire for death or she could try to develop the skill to receive these powerful energies without them burning her up and destroying her. The magic that they held was beyond her mind's comprehension. She would have to become bigger than her mind, than her body. She would have to enter into the vast expanse of nothingness that contained everything, that held all and more than could ever be known.

She felt her body open, break apart, disappear. The afternoon light took on a dark metallic hue, the forms became translucent blue flame. They entered where her body had been. She became the blueness. It was warm and cool at the same time.

And then the unspeaking voices rang clear. They told her, "This is your path." Life was not finished with her. She must stay. She had work to do. She must soon go and find the Sangoma and begin her training. This was her calling. She must learn well and become the link between the Ancestors and those in pain, to be the instrument for their healing. She must heal herself, learn humility, undergo purification, wash in the blood of the sacrificial goat and partake of the sacred Muti to align with the spirits, to enter again and again into the crack in the earth. She was to seek the wisdom, to withstand the wisdom, to yield and to step aside from her own self to allow the wisdom.

Slowly the wind subsided, her body returned and the voices departed. The earth resealed itself, and the dry, red earth reappeared. She now knew that she had no choice. It was no longer her will but the will of the Ancestors that guided her life. She turned, knowing that all her footsteps from now on would lead her along the path her grandmother had always forseen.

Ntombi walked back towards her grandmother's hut. She paused, sensing Gogo was hovering on the border of this life and beyond. She turned to go and get Gosololo but she was already there walking toward her.

"Yes," Gosololo said, "I heard the call."

The two of them quietly entered Gogo's hut, their eyes slowly adjusting to the soft dimness. They sat on either side of her mat settling into their vigil. Ntombi watched the tentative rise and fall of her grandmother's chest, heard the halting breath, felt the presence of her mother and father. Something shifted. Gogo's breath seemed endless. All Ntombi's senses became alert as she realized the importance of this breath. She looked at her grandmother and watched her body slacken, soften, her face dropping, her eyes reflecting the grey light of the open portal inviting her in. The breath that barely held her earth-bound now lifted her into beyond. No final glance. Her direction only forward, this last breath releasing the anchor of her life, freeing her. Ntombi continued to watch long after the silence settled, her mind empty.

Gosololo slowly rose, went to the cooling body and taking the palm of its left hand pressed it to her own forehead. She held it there for a few moments, her lips moving in a quiet prayer. She gently replaced the hand and left the hut. Ntombi remained, empty, no tears, unable to move. After some time, Gosololo returned, took Ntombi by the hand and led her out of the hut.

"Come now, child, we will prepare together for the burial."

Ntombi looked up into Gosololo's face. "It is too much for me. I am not strong enough."

Gosololo felt a twinge of fear race through her. She knew this place inside her own self. "Allow your pain to feed you, do not let it destroy you. Trust in the unknown hands that are guiding you. One day you will understand. For now, your only task is to stay alive."

Once again the village gathered in the burial ritual. Once again they asked the Ancestors to receive the spirit of the departed. Once again they asked for the healing of Ntombi's spirit.

After the ritual was complete and Gogo had been buried and the fire which consumed some cuttings of her hair had burned out, Ntombi entered Gogo's hut. She looked around. She smelled Gogo everywhere, a sweet, dusty smell. She sat down on Gogo's sleeping mat, worn smooth from the many years of her life, that life now gone like smoke, threading its way through the thick humid air to the sky. That life now beginning among the Ancestors, rejoining Ntombi's mother. Ntombi felt them both holding her from the other side. She lowered her eyes to the mud floor and watched an ant scurrying with a load in its mouth.

When she was a little girl, her mother always used to say, "Watch those ants now, they know how to work. No one has to tell them what to do, they just know. They understand they each have their task and all are needed. Remember that, Ntombi, everything you do has purpose and it must be for the good of all." Ntombi could see her mother's soft eyes, could feel her cool, firm hand pressed into the hand of her younger self as she passed Ntombi's hand to Gogo and then faded into nothing. Gogo's hand felt rough and thick, full of heat and strength. Ntombi grabbed hold of Gogo's hand with both her little hands, holding on, holding on tighter as Gogo's hands grew cold and disintegrated into ashes that fell through her fingers.

Ntombi's body jerked. She looked around the hut once more, rose from the mat and, taking the pouch tied to her waist, opened it and smeared some of Gogo's ashes on the walls of the hut. She rubbed in circles until the grey ash blended with the dried brown mud and there was no separation between Gogo and the walls that had housed her. Ntombi pressed her forehead to the wall. The walls were cool. Her tears were hot. She ran her tongue along the mud and ash, taking Gogo's life and death into her body. She knew her bond with the Ancestors was strengthened now that Gogo was with them. But even so, she felt alone and afraid.

She took a deep breath, lifted her head from the wall, brushed her tears aside with the traces of Gogo's ashes still on her fingertips. She walked to the door of the hut, her eyes taking in the brilliance of the light, and she walked through the opening. She didn't look back.

Ntombi walked towards Gosololo's hut where she now stayed. She had had no heart left to be in the hut she once shared with Gogo. As she approached the hut, splintered rainbows in jagged shapes appeared everywhere she looked. She knew what would follow, the nausea, the blinding pain knotted behind her right eye. Before its full force hit, she entered Gosololo's hut and lay on the earth, grateful that the ground would hold her for the duration of yet another onslaught. These bouts were happening more and more often, each time the intensity increasing. No herbs or elixirs seemed to alter its course. Ntombi sensed the truth behind these headaches but stubbornly tried to explain them away in the hopes that she was wrong.

When she was able to resurface, she walked out of the hut into the waning daylight. Gosololo was waiting for her, "Your grandmother spoke to me often of your calling and you must know by now that the time has arrived for you to follow. There will be no relief for you until you do. You know it is your resistance to your path that causes your pain."

"I know," Ntombi wept quietly. "I am afraid. I do not want to go."

"Trust them, child. The Ancestors have chosen you for a reason and you must heed their call."

"I know," Ntombi said softly, "but I am still afraid."

"Then let your fear be your fuel." Gosololo pulled Ntombi into her. "Gogo is now among the Ancestors. She is there to help you."

INTO THE VELD

N tombi walked out into the veld. The moon was just rising, full and round. The colours of the land were starting to melt. She gazed across the land, this beautiful land that held all her Ancestors, that held all her sorrows and her joys. Ntombi sat down and began to weep. Why did the Ancestors call her this way? She did not want to enter into their mystery, even though she knew to enter would free her. She didn't know if she wanted this freedom, for who would she be if not the familiar story of her history? Who would she be if she stepped into a new self? And yet, her heart ached for freedom. The endless weight on her soul was old and tired, asking to be released. Ntombi could taste the sweet possibility of new life but her fear of stepping through the veil between known and unknown, past and future was great. She felt alone. There was no one she could turn to for guidance. In her heart, she feared that if she surrendered to the will of the Ancestors, she would be destined to be alone forever.

She lay on the orange earth, feeling the warmth that it still held from the day infuse her body. The call of the Ancestors was strong. Her fear was strong. She was tired of the pull between the two. She closed her eyes and wept. Her tears mingled with the earth. The land held her as she slipped into sleep. As she stepped into the dreamtime Gogo came to her and enfolded her in her arms, stroking her hair. Ntombi felt the warmth and comfort of her grandmother's love. She slept deeply, the kind of weightless sleep that penetrates into the marrow of the bones and heals.

Ntombi began to climb back to consciousness just as she entered crystal time, that crossover space between asleep and awake. She saw a brilliant double rainbow, two full arcs of vibrant distinct colours. It took her breath away, and just as her mind was beginning to form around the vision, it vanished. She woke fully to the cool of the night. The moon had traveled high towards the heavens. The stars were crisp. The moon was encircled in a double ring of rainbow light. She sat up.

"I am from a long line of strong women. I am from the dust of my mother's bones, from the breath of my grandmother's lungs. They are my earth and my air. I am from a long line of strong men. I am from the sweat of my father's body, from the smell of my grandfather's smoke. They are my blood and my spirit. Their lives, their deaths inform my walking on the earth. I hear their voices guiding me...these four and beyond, stretching back into unseen corners of time and space. My Ancestors call to me and point the way. 'Be not afraid, trust the steps you take,' they tell me. 'You are never alone.' And when I peer at the path ahead, I feel their strong proud shoulders touching my own, and fear dissolves into the lake of distant memory. I feel their muscles moving me forward, their strength firm, carrying me to my work in the world."

Perhaps her fear would return, but for now she was clear. She would surrender to the will of the Ancestors. She returned to the village knowing that with the morning light she would make her way, following as the Ancestors directed.

That night in a dream the Ancestors came to her again, took her hand and showed her the way to the woman who was destined to be her teacher. It was a long way off. After waking, Ntombi went to Gogo's grave. She took a small twig from the nearby Buffalo Thorn tree and knelt down by the mound of earth holding her grandmother's bones and ashes. She asked the spirit of her grandmother to enter the leaves and stem so Ntombi could have Gogo with her during her journey and her training.

She then collected some white heather and went to Gogo's hut. She had not entered it for some time. She looked at the walls, still alive with her childhood, her child's childhood and Gogo's life and death. She set the twigs alight and when the smoke rose she cupped it in both hands and directed it around her head and shoulders. She bowed her head toward the ground. She informed the Ancestors that she would be leaving the village to seek her teacher and that she did not know when she might return. She asked them to accompany and protect her on her journey.

Ntombi returned to Gosololo in her hut and gathered a few things: her drinking gourd, a sack of biltong and dried fruit, the amulet her great-grandmother had worn and her walking stick. The two women faced each other. Gosololo pulled Ntombi into a full embrace, not knowing if she would ever see this splendid girl again. Gosololo willed all her love and protection into Ntombi's strong frame.

"Watch your fear," Gosololo said. "It can be your friend or your enemy. Listen to it carefully and trust your path."

Ntombi drank in the full love of this big-hearted woman. How fortunate she had been to have not one, but two strong, wise women to mould and guide her life. Even though they could never fill the emptiness left by her mother's death, Ntombi knew she had been blessed. She pulled away and smiled into the old woman's eyes.

"Thank you, Gosololo, for everything," she said.

As Ntombi walked through the village, some of the children fell in line behind her, skipping and laughing. But as Ntombi reached the gate, they became quiet. Sensing something was different, they looked at her with questioning eyes.

"Be gentle with one another," Ntombi said, as she playfully pinched their cheeks. She walked through the gate without looking back, but felt the gaze of Gosololo and the children as she followed the path.

After a few hours of walking, Ntombi stopped to rest. She sat on a low rock and took a measured sip of water. She took out a piece of biltong and, with her teeth, repeatedly massaged the dried meat until it released its salty flavour. She swallowed, savouring its rich taste.

She looked at the land stretching far into the distance and felt a deep loneliness. Picking up her things she resumed her walk, feeling the tug of sadness close at her heels. As night approached, she stopped to eat some dried berries and drink some more water. She sat and waited...for what, she didn't know. As the light changed, her body began to slowly move to a rhythm that was strangely familiar. She released herself into the movement, carried further and further into a whirling that lifted her off her seat and round and round in a joyous and torturous frenzy. Time was suspended as she continued to dance until she sank, spent, onto the ground.

Ntombi lay there, her body and mind in a slow deep trance, the hysteria of the dance now transformed into complete stillness. Her senses pulled into the centre of her core. Time dissolved, sight diminished, sensation softened. A sound entered her awareness – a soft, full, continuous hum that seemed to contain all sound. As she became immersed in the sound, her fear dissolved. She trusted that whatever her destiny was to be, she would be led to it. The Ancestors knew her course. She did not need to know it. Her task was to surrender and allow it. She settled there inside the sound and even joy now became a part of it.

As Ntombi crossed the stretch of veld and reached the transition between flat and hill she came upon an *isivivane*, the large pile of stones. It radiated warmth as she approached. She felt the aspirations, the will and desires of all those who had passed this way as they piled their chosen rock upon the others left by fellow travelers.

She paused, feeling the bottoms of her feet where they connected with the dry grass. She took a deep breath, closed her eyes and heard the long exhale as the air slowly left her body. She felt the weariness of the day's walk draining into the earth as she exhaled. She opened her eyes and looked left and then right, her gaze coming to rest on a rock that was the size of her palm. She walked over to it and, as tradition dictated, curled the toes of her left foot around it. Its sharp points pressed into her skin. She bent her knee to the side as she stooped to transfer the rock to her right hand. She felt the warmth of the day's sun that was infused in it travel up her left leg, up her right arm, throughout her body until it united in the centre of her chest. She walked back to stand in front of the pile of stones and, placing her lips and some saliva on the stone in her hand, gave thanks to the local spirits for the beauty of the land and asked for safety to successfully travel along her unknown path. She placed the stone on top of the heap of others, thanking those who had gone before. It was a great comfort to know that others were on their journey, wherever it would take them, and she called on their successes and failures to teach her and to guide her.

Wandiswe

Ntombi traveled for many days and nights with the small twig from the Buffalo Thorn tree carefully wrapped in a pouch that hung around her neck, close to her heart. She reached the crest of a hill and at the far side of the valley in front of her was a river. Beyond the river, a village sprawled up a hillside. This was the village she had seen in her dream.

She placed her hand around the pouch. Her heartbeat was loud in her ears. There was a fluttering in her chest. She walked forward. The footpath was warm and dusty, the fine, red dust splashing over her naked feet, the warmth from the day's sun flowing from the earth through her soles. As she approached the village a crow appeared, circling over her head. The bird flew away from the village and up to a bend in the river. It returned to Ntombi, circled again and again and flew up to the bend in the river. Ntombi followed. Just past the bend was a grove of lidloti trees with sacks hanging from their branches. Beside the trees was a lone hut. Her brow began to soften, the anxiety and anticipation giving way to the calm energy radiating from the hut. As she approached it her pace slowed. She paused before the dark opening, feeling its pull, knowing that once she crossed over into its inner sanctuary, she would leave outside a former self that could never be reclaimed. She breathed in the air of the beloved land, filling herself. She heard a woman's steady voice… "Enter", it said. Ntombi bowed her head and stepped through the opening to meet her teacher.

Wandiswe smiled at Ntombi. "I have been waiting for you," she said. "the Ancestors are glad you have come. Come and sit. We will throw the bones. Let us begin."

And so began seven years of training.

COMPLETION

Seven years had passed since Ntombi had stepped into her new life. Her teacher Wandiswe was at various turns harsh, gentle, impatient, compassionate. Ntombi had passed through many trials and rituals, her connection to the Ancestors tested over and over again, at times grueling, at times blissful, a relentless exploration of deeper and deeper mysteries.

The time had come to follow her teacher into the veld. Once again Ntombi drank the harsh-tasting potion knowing it would send spasms of pain throughout her gut. She heard the silence in her teacher's footsteps as she followed her through the grasses and over the rocks. Wandiswe was like a sleek animal making its way through the bush... there, but invisible unless you had eyes to see. The surefooted placement of each step was precise and effortless, while Ntombi stumbled along behind her. Seven years she had been training and still she felt deeply inadequate; sure that the Ancestors had been mistaken in calling her, overestimating her abilities. The old doubts had crept back in, obscuring her concentration. She no longer knew what was coming before it came. The blinding pain behind her right eye had returned and no amount of willing it away had been successful.

The taste of metal was in her mouth. Her sight was a mass of splintered rainbows outlining the shapes along the path. Her stomach churned and twisted. Her foot caught yet another rock and she lurched forward, her face grinding through the dust, pierced by sharp flint. Blood mixed with red dirt making a thick dark clay. Her left wrist, bent at a wrong angle, shot with pain where she had attempted to stay her fall. The sting of tears. She pushed up onto her knees and retched from deep in her belly, emptying everything from her insides.

When her body calmed, she looked up to see Wandiswe seated nearby on a rock. Ntombi obeyed the silent hand signal for her to rise and follow. She winced with each step, her knees weak and bloodied, her cheek open and raw. She was not strong enough for this path. She wanted it to end.

They walked on toward the approaching night. Wandiswe turned off the path. Ntombi followed her through the scrub and reeds to the river. She felt the sure grip of Wandiswe's hand guiding her into the middle of the river until the cool of the water reached her ribs. Then with the next step the bottom disappeared. Ntombi surrendered to the force of Wandiswe's hands pressing on her shoulders. Her knees buckled and her body submerged. Liquid light covered her face and head. Her body sank like a stone, falling, falling through space and time. All the air left her lungs with one exhale. There had been too much pain, too much loss, too much doubt, too many times rising out of the depths. She had no will to rise again. She felt the water around her limbs, the faint flavour of her mother's womb... go back to mother now... safe...leave this life...breathe in the river... let it take you back to mother...leave this torment and doubt... be done with it...rest inside mother. Ntombi's lungs started to fill with water, landing heavy and foreign in her body, a mixture of pleasure and panic. She willed the panic to recede. She was done, finished with all of it. A black hole appeared, expanding as she surrendered to it. Annihilation.

From deep within the black fog, her Great Grandmother emerged, the amber amulet glowing at her throat. At one side of her was Gogo, at the other side, Lindiwe, the mothers who had carried her thus far.

"Is this where you end?" she heard, floating in the dark. "We are calling you, asking you to choose carefully. You look for Mother now in Death. Mother is also in Life. We are calling you. Find us in Life. To abandon your gift is to waste it and all you have prepared for, and all that we have lived and died for. Choose."

Ntombi's limbs twitched as her life force receded, her will watching it fade. A flash exploded from the amulet. Her legs kicked and her arms pulled down, over and over, propelling her up to the surface of the water. She spluttered, gasping, while the air competed for space in lungs heavy with fluid.

Wandiswe grabbed Ntombi and spun her around, pulling Ntombi's back close and wrapping her arms around the front of her thrashing body. In quick jerking motions she pulled her arms in and up, forcing the remaining water from Ntombi's lungs. Once she heard Ntombi's breath returning to its regular rhythm, she released her grip and came to stand before her. She cupped water with both her hands and slowly poured it over Ntombi's head. She repeated this three times. As the water released and trickled down Ntombi's face, neck and body, Wandiswe's hands followed the trail of water. As her fingers touched the torn flesh, Ntombi began to weep. Ntombi wept for her mother's hands, gone so long ago, her gentle mother whose bones had been burned to dust. She wept for Gogo's hands that had taken the place of her mother's. She wept for her Great Grandmother's hands that had learned the ways of healing. She wept for Wandiswe's hands that had held her through her training. She felt all these hands moving across her skin again and again. Gradually her pain began to soften and fall away.

Together they walked out of the water. Wandiswe raised her hands, palms turned skyward, face lifted for a moment then she bent to the ground and gathered three handfuls of white heather from beside the river. She placed them in her sack.

Ntombi followed her teacher and together they made their way along the riverbank until Wandiswe made a sharp turn to the left. Ntombi had seen no marker, no change in landscape to announce the change of direction but once they turned she saw a faint narrow band of light on the ground that, as her eyes followed it, stretched across the savannah and up through hills of rock.

They walked on as the sky began to change, the horizon a band of pale blue layered above with soft pinks and mauves. The air smelled of earth and grass, sweet and dusty. It smelled of heat releasing from rock with a fading damp smell from the river.

They walked on, the horizon now a burnt orange, blue riding above its edge and deepening into the vast blue of approaching night. They walked on, the dark increasing, the sky becoming crowded with stars. And still they followed the gentle band of light as it wound its way around and up and over boulders and earth. Ntombi reached out her hand onto rocks to steady herself as she maneuvered the complicated terrain. Her breath laboured, and, in spite of the cool night, lines of sweat trickled down her arms, her back and her legs. If she had not seen Wandiswe's outline ahead she would never have known she was still there, so quiet was her breath and footfall.

And then Ntombi saw it...the glow lifting from the ground and spreading to each side, revealing a massive rock face. As they drew near, the rock seemed to dissolve exposing a large cave.

Wandiswe climbed up to a ledge at the entrance of the cave. She stopped at the entrance. Taking the water skin from her shoulder, she tipped some water into her left hand, took a sip, swished it around in her mouth and released it over the ledge into the night. She smoothed the water that remained in her palm over her head. She touched her palm to her forehead, her throat and then her heart. She gestured to Ntombi to do the same.

Ntombi felt the precious water inside her mouth and refused the impulse to swallow it. Instead she repeated as Wandiswe had done and spat it out in the ritual of purification.

Together they walked through the thin veil of light into the dark. Wandiswe took the white heather from her sack and set it alight. She knelt beside it and waved the sacred smoke over her head and shoulders. She motioned to Ntombi to come and do the same. Together they sat on the ground facing the night.

Soon Ntombi's eyelids began to droop. She was tired from the long walk and could feel sleep creeping into her senses, dulling her awareness. Suddenly, and with more noise than Ntombi had heard from her all day, Wandiswe rose and said, "I will wait for you outside the cave. Do not come out until it is time." Then she was gone.

Ntombi was now wide awake and afraid. She knew something was coming and she trembled. She did not have the will or the strength to face any more this night. She looked around the cave barely lit by the burning heather. Small branches and sticks of wood were stacked near the entrance. She brought them to the smoldering fire and breaking off the small pieces, added them to the embers, building up a base of flame before adding the larger pieces. The flames grew as the wood caught and settled into a steady burn. Warmth entered her tired limbs. She sat gazing into the fire, soothed by the familiar flickering of its light.

Her eyes followed the sparks as they danced up into the air lifting her gaze to hover above the flames. There, through sounds of wood crackling and popping, through sparks appearing and disappearing, shapes appeared on the walls. The light played upon the images making them shift and sway: kudu, wildebeest, giraffe, zebra, baboon, man, some distinct and separate, some layered, some overlapping, all moving together in an endless procession echoing through time and space. The womb of rock pulsated with life, ancient souls murmuring, their stories holding her inside this sacred space. She was safe.

She lay her body on the earth, resting on bones now turned to dust, soft and comfortable. She slipped into sleep, into the dreamtime, down through the years, back to then.

She is in the transition hut. It is night, dark and black. She almost hears a sound, on alert now, waiting to understand the source of her fear. She blinks, then heavy hand against her mouth, foul breath against her face, low growl vibrating through her bones. Another hand fumbling over breast, moving over torso, ripping at her private place, knees jamming thighs apart, flash of pain, insides breaking. This time her teeth grow large and sink into that hand, sink deep tearing flesh down to the bone. Her arms and legs push and dislodge the heaving body. She fights, she scratches, she kicks, she punches, she screams and she screams and she screams.

She woke to the sounds of her screams reverberating around the walls of the cave, around and around and around, deafening. The cave spat out the sound into the night, into the air, into the landscape, up into the endless sky, down into the bottomless earth, no longer hers to carry. Her body began to twitch and jerk, releasing spasms of memory. Pain seared through the muscles of arms and legs, paralysed with fear so many years ago. Her body continued to shudder, the evil that had been implanted shaking its way out of her limbs. Pain everywhere as her body strained and stretched, darkness moving through sinew and bone. Then, slowly, a sensation like warm honey crept through her, filling every space, every nerve, every fibre, every cell, every heartbeat. Her breath became soft and quiet.

The fire had gone out but she was not cold. There was no light in the cave but it was not dark.

Ntombi sat, her back straight, her body relaxing. She closed her eyes and sensed only the in-and-out of her breath. Her body became weightless. Behind her eyelids was filled with rich, vibrant indigo. She travelled with the stars.

Here she remained until the gentle sound of a wooden flute summoned her back to her body. She listened, entranced, as one note bent and curled into the next. Deep, low sound gathering and spiraling to high sweet trills calling her, calling her back. It was time. She opened her eyes, the coloured light of dawn at the mouth of the cave illuminating the sacred symbols that had watched over her through the dark night. She bowed low in gratitude, thanking the Ancestors for safely guiding her on her way. She trusted she would be able now to greet her fear as a friend who was there to lead her into the depths of her terror and usher her to the other side of that dark to sturdier ground. She had found a different way to be with fear.

She rose and bowed once more to the womb of rock, turned to the dawning of the day and left the cave. The land waited in hushed tones for the sun to appear. Ntombi climbed the rocks with ease, her body fluid and sure. She saw Wandiswe perched on a rock, her face gentle in the growing light. As she was on her way to her, Ntombi turned, went in the other direction and began collecting brush and wood, as much as her arms could carry. She retraced her steps up to the magnificent cave and respectfully piled them just inside the entrance. She turned once again toward her teacher.

As Ntombi approached, Wandiswe rose and smiled, and when they were standing face-to-face Wandiswe placed her right hand over her heart and her left hand over Ntombi's heart.

"You have found your voice in the face of fear and the power to act, but there is more to come."

Over the next months Wandiswe continued to teach and test Ntombi, having her make mixtures and poultices for those who sought relief from belly aches, headaches, infertility, and all manner of ailments. She taught her how to throw and read the bones, to know how best to banish evil spirits and release demons from those possessed. Wandiswe would hide objects and instruct Ntombi to find them. Ntombi learned how to pull all her senses inside, become very still and wait until she felt their vibration, then follow the invisible light that led to their hiding place.

"You have learned well," Wandiswe said to Ntombi. "And there is more darkness you need to enter."

Ntombi felt the familiar flash of fear and tried to let it roll over her as she breathed. As night approached Ntombi followed Wandiswe out into the veld. Together they assembled a ring of stones and started a small fire within it. So long ago Ntombi had left her village with its sweet smell of grasses, the earthy smell of Gogo, the wet smell of the river. Now, as she stood in front of her teacher, the invitation to step through into more of the unknown was both terrifying and exhilarating. It was as if this moment had always been predetermined, irrevocable, her own will never significant.

Wandiswe held up a simple carved wooden bowl, the liquid inside murky and opaque. It smelled of fear, of death. Ntombi stared into the darkness of Wandiswe's eyes. A pulsing began at the base of her spine and, beat by beat, traveled its way up to her throat, behind her eyes to the top of her head. Trickling sparks traced down her arms to her fingertips, an intense aliveness spreading everywhere.

She took the cup and lifted it to her lips. The cool liquid slipped through her mouth, down her throat, she felt it move down, down to below her belly where it caught fire…rumbling, churning, swelling, rising. The muscles along her spine tightened. Her stomach clenched and contractions rippled and radiated from deep in her gut. Her mouth was thick with saliva. Waves upon waves of nausea rose and waned, rose again. Her belly concaved and her back rounded. Undigested viscous chunks rolled upward, erupting into the night, splashing onto stones and dust.

Ntombi's head was pounding, her eyes wet and strained. Her body shivered, sweat seeped though her pores, cold and hot. Another wave, another unstoppable eruption. Slime dripped from her mouth. She fell to her knees, a violent scream piercing the night. Sparks from the fire cracked and flew high, bursting into images of splintered bones and burning flesh. Scenes from the night of the Great Fire danced in her head in a crazy deafening sound of screams and burning thatch.

Demons rose in the air, then dove down and entered her body, twisting limbs and pushing the insides of her belly to bursting. Hlwelo's face flashed before her. His body formed and thrust itself against her flesh, once again insisting its way into her, ripping open her woman place. This time a force of rage roared in her ears. Her hand fumbled for the ground and found a stone. Her fingers clawed around it. She heaved it above her head and clasping it in both hands brought it crashing down on Hlwelo's head, blow after blow, the sound of splintering skull, the splashing of warm blood raining down covering her face, running in her eyes, her mouth, her ears. She spat his blood back in his face and continued pummeling his body until it became an unmoving red mass of dead weight. She ripped his penis from his groin and mashed it over and over with the bloodied rock. She tore at his limbs and with the force of ten bull elephants ripped the arms from their sockets, legs from the pelvis and flung them wide into the night. Lungs, heart ripped from their cage of bones, teeth sank into intestines, blood and bile running down her neck.

She shrieked a high-pitched, rolling laugh. Fire danced around her and the carnage, flames consuming Hlwelo's bones and flesh. The fire leapt and sparked until it had spent all the fuel, then spluttered and shrank, returning the night to the dark.

It was deadly quiet. Ntombi opened her eyes. She was standing, legs apart, firm on the ground, sweat streaking her body. She saw the quiet ring of stones encircling a gentle fire.

Wandiswe was standing on the other side of the fire. She nodded.

"It is important that you know this rage and murder," she said, "for without knowing it in your own body first you can never understand it in another, and if you cannot understand it you can be of no help. These demons demand respect, and no one is above them or without them. And for one to think one does not have them dwelling in their own being is where true danger lies. We are all the same. We are all made up of everything. We all carry destruction, just as we all carry love. It is your path to assist people to recognize the first and to cultivate the second."

Ntombi nodded, no voice left inside her.

Wandiswe smiled, "Now you are ready for your name."

Wandiswe assembled a band of Sangomas as witness and to administer the tests necessary for Ntombi to undergo in order to complete her training. Sangomas, both men and women, came from across the land. Each Sangoma hid an article and one by one Ntombi found each one and returned it to its rightful owner. Together they lit the fire, each having brought a branch from their homestead to add to the flames. They sat in a circle around the fire, united in the journey they shared into the Great Mystery, each in their own silent contemplation, solitary in their unique expression of it. It was midnight before Ntombi heard the whisper. The moon had disappeared beyond the hill. The wind began to dance. It grew from a ripple of music into sizzling thunder. The chant of the Ancestors swirled around her. Red cinders flew from the fire into the night. She saw the flashes of her Ancestors. Her bones shivered. She began to dance a slow rhythmic beat, her feet stamping the earth, her arms lifting and falling.

"Hay-ahhh, hay-ahhh," her throat sang. "Hay-ahhh, Hay-ahhh."

She began to swirl, the light from the flames illuminating her in the darkness. The wind carried her voice into the veld. The land listened, waited, captivated by the guttural sound of the fire in her blood joining with the breath of the Ancestors. The wind returned from the veld and entered her. Mfundi, the sound resonated through her. Mfundi, she heard then sang it out loud, feeling its echo as it resounded into the air.

The eyes of her mentor were shining. Ntombi felt her new name, Mfundi: scholar, student, disciple. She would always be a disciple to the ways of the Great Mystery, always learning, studying, going deeper. In gratitude, she looked at her teacher. She had spent these years with her, learning the secrets of the herbs, plants and barks, learning to open and purify her body, learning to open her mind and her spirit to the wisdom of the Ancestors, learning the ways of the Sangoma. They smiled at one another, the warmth of their time together firmly secured in their bodies, surrounded now by the circle of healers who had assembled for this naming ritual.

Wandiswe handed Mfundi a sturdy staff. Mfundi felt the carved *tamboti* wood under her hand and admired the colours; deep brown joined seamlessly alongside honey yellow. How had the Gods decided to combine two such opposing shades in one strong tree? The staff had been carved for her by her Wandiswe's teacher, generations of ancestral connection held within each curve.

The Sangomas rose and surrounded Mfundi. They draped long circular strands of colourful beads around her body, criss-crossing them across her chest and shoulders, and crossing again against her back to represent and confirm the connection that dispels all duality of left and right, male and female. They tied other strands around her waist, wrists and ankles. Each Sangoma had brought something, their spirit and power infusing the beads and threads. They enveloped her in a zebra skin. Their voices lifted, the women's ululations clear and strong, the men's *Hau!* welcoming her. She entered into their company, thanking the Ancestors and the Gods for choosing her and allowing her to join them.

Ntombi felt the strength in the cape around her body. She was ready now to step into that for which she had been training. She stepped into Mfundi.

It was now time for Mfundi to go into the veld alone and perform her private ritual. She felt the sturdy staff under her hand. She made her way to the top of the *kopje* and collected a series of stones, each one carefully chosen according to the vibration she felt while holding it in her hands. Each stone sang to her of earth, of sky, of water, of smoke. She carefully arranged them into a circle. This ceremony was for her and her alone to sanctify the lessons that she held in her heart, the zebra skin draped over her shoulders, the staff she carried that defined her status.

In the weeks leading up to her initiation, she had gathered resin from the umsulusulu trees, mixed it with earth and herbs and molded it into nests. She took these now from the pouch tied at her waist. She placed them in the circle of stones beginning with one to the south, the place of beginnings; one to the north where the four winds meet; one to the east, the place of illumination; and one to the west, the place of darkness, introspection, where one enters the silence ready to listen and receive. Then she added the rest of the nests, filling in the circle.

She opened various other leather pouches and sprinkled bark, dried plant leaves, and incense over the whole circle. She lit the centre and watched as the fire licked its way to the edges, flames dancing, fragrant smoke wafting up to the Gods. She began a dance, the strands of large red, green, black and white beads crossing from each shoulder to and around her waist, the strands of blue and white beads around her ankles and wrists creating a cascade of sound with each step. She pounded the earth with her staff. Her pace quickened, the raspy voice of her chief Ancestor flying from her throat, singing, rejoicing. For hours she danced, her beads sliding in her sweat, until she slowed her pace. She regained her body from the Ancestors. With her staff, she drew circles in the quiet fire, and a reignited flame followed the path of the designs she made. She sat by the stone circle, bowed her head and thanked the Ancestors for choosing her, for guiding her to her destiny through pain, loss and broken dreams, for bringing her to this spot, to this circle of stones, to who she was meant to be: a Sangoma.

HLWELO'S JOURNEY

In the years since he had left the village, Hlwelo had traveled far, moving through the veld, avoiding human contact whenever possible. He hunted and cooked his food as he went. Nyongo had taught him well in spite of his sullen unwillingness to learn. But out there he had had to become alert.

He recalled the apprenticeship at his father's side, watching carefully the melting of rock and refashioning it into hunting tools. At first Hlwelo's attempts were rough, weighty, misshapen. But with time and persistence he learned the art of refining and balancing his spears. It became one of the only moments of relief from his anger and despair, to sit and repeatedly rub a stone against the flat of the spearhead creating a sure, sharp point.

He practiced throwing his spear, picking out targets as his father had done so many years before, placing his body at just the correct angle, focusing his attention and then thrusting all his hate with the shaft and watching it slice through the air to find its chosen destination. He became an accurate marksman. Mostly he hunted impala and springbok, as they were plentiful and relatively easy to find. He would smell the air, catch the scent of his prey, scour the ground for evidence of their path, a cracked twig, a bent blade of grass, and he would follow, silent in his pursuit. He had watched how larger animals preyed on smaller. He sought out the weak and the young in the herd. He was strategic and decisive once he had chosen, as these were quick animals and startled easily.

He would go in for the kill from just the right angle, finding the exact location on the body to plunge the spear to sever the main artery, then watch the crumple of legs, hear the thud of halted body hitting the ground, see the dust rise as the beast landed, hear the last breaths grunting from dying lungs. He would skin and carve up the deer quickly, roast some strips of the flesh over a fire to eat his fill, set some strips out to dry in the sun to take with him and leave the rest for the jackals and vultures to pick clean.

Sometimes he would watch the sky and look for circling vultures knowing they were waiting for their turn above some kill. He would follow them in the hopes of claiming some leftovers, being careful to be sure whoever the killer had been had already vacated the area.

He collected berries and dug roots, trapped insects. He especially liked the crickets and grasshoppers. They were tricky to trap but tasted so good when cooked over a fire, their bodies crispy in his mouth.

In times when water was scarce, in the early mornings he would sip the dew that had collected in crevices where the leaves of plants converged. He would turn rocks over and wait for dew to form and lick it off. He would dig to the roots of trees and suck the moisture from them. If there were grubs in the roots he would eat those for what little moisture their bodies contained, in spite of their gritty texture and sour taste. The grubs also showed him that the tree was rotten. He would then harvest the tree for firewood, for he was careful to never take a live tree. Although he seemed to carry distain for any human life, including his own, he had a deep respect for the land and all that was on it, the grasses, the trees, the shrubs, the animals, the water. Whenever water was plentiful he would fill his sack and his hollowed out ostrich eggs. He would bury the eggs to be assured of having water if he should return that way.

Sometimes when he found berries, after a few bites he would remember it was while collecting berries that his mother had been taken by the white man, and the taste would sour in his mouth. His life had been destroyed by his mother for giving him birth, by Dinzane for killing his father, by Ntombi for driving him to violate her, but most of all by the white man who had forced the beginning of his life into his mother. He was always the white man in his mind, never his father. For to have thought of him that way would have meant he was a part of him.

He could never forgive this beast for being the cause of his abhorrent form. He wanted to hunt this white man down and torture him mercilessly for condemning him to a life of humiliation and isolation. But Hlwelo knew he would never be able to find him to take his revenge and ease his torment. He was doomed to walk the days of his life in hatred and bitterness. Sometimes at night when he couldn't sleep, he wondered if this white man ever questioned whether the seeds that he had left had taken root, that somewhere walking the earth there might be someone, a disgusting example of his arrogance, someone not a beautiful shiny black but a dirty, muddled white colour, not wanted anywhere.

Whenever anyone happened to see Hlwelo it seemed as if he vanished and a legend grew of a white phantom haunting the land. Stories were spun around the fires at night and children huddled in terror at their telling.

Hlwelo lived in isolation, his heart sealed. And yet, every now and then some small thing would seep its way through a seam in his chest: a glint of light on a river, a lioness licking off the birth blood from her newborn cubs, a *umzwilili* bird calling to the dawn, and he would feel … what… something… tenderness? sadness? These gentle, quiet feelings frightened him and he would quickly seal them over once again. Over time they became more frequent and he was less able to control them. These soft sensations eventually began to erode the covering to his heart, in the same way an insistent droplet of water can reshape a rock. Desperation crept into his wandering and he moved faster and faster from one spot to another as if pursued.

He had been comfortable with his hard ways. His bitterness was his companion. But now he was distraught. There was a devil of gentleness inside him that tore at his spirit. His body ached with pains in his chest and his groin. His mind began to shatter. Frightening shapes appeared and disappeared. Strange sounds built to a deafening pitch then subsided. He was going mad. He knew it.

Hlwelo settled down for the night in the wilderness, but no rest came. He sat by the fire until it burned down to almost nothing and the day began to dawn. The wind scattered the ashes, lifting them up into the sky. Hlwelo watched the grey particles swirl, lift, fall, disappear. It was cold in the early light. He lowered his hands, hovering them above the coals still burning from last night's fire. His palms welcomed the heat. He closed his eyes, his thoughts drifted back to his village, to his childhood when young and old alike would gather round the fire and first the men would dance and then the women. The first time he saw her dance at the harvest celebration was the first time his body was no longer a boy's but a man's, with the thrill and terror of desire. Waves of heat had pulsed through him as he watched her body move, her feet stomping, dust rising, hands slapping thighs, the smacking sound of flesh against flesh. The fire cast haunting shadows that undulated across her body. Of all the girls in the village he saw only her, the tight curl of her black hair close to her finely-shaped head, the swinging of beads as they clacked together with each turn of her full hips, the ripple of breast as each foot landed with precision.

Hlwelo opened his eyes, the flesh of his hands burning as they pressed through the ash to the glowing embers beneath. He ground his teeth, snorting out a derisive laugh. His hands deserved to be burned, scarred forever; not enough punishment for touching her, for ruining her. He looked to the pale sky, tears falling down his face. A black raven circled above his head, once, twice, three times and flew towards the east. Hlwelo wiped his eyes, the grey ash blending with his pale skin. He got up from his knees and gathered his water skin and spear. He followed in the direction of the raven. He had lost any confidence in his own abilities and now gave himself over to any omen that might lead him to his fate.

Hlwelo's body was like lead. Something was clawing around his heart, ripping around the edges, trying to unearth something buried. He pushed down these sensations, trying to crush them only to have them re-emerge from beneath the force of his will. He had lost control of his mind and his body. He was so tired. Looking out over the land, he did not see its beauty, the subtleties of the colours. He did not feel the softness of the breeze.

His gaze fixed on a maze of rocks stacked jagged and high. The raven was circling above it. As if in a trance, lifting out of the struggle in his body with his feet barely touching the ground, he moved to the mountain and began his ascent. He didn't see the sensuous curves of the stone or feel the heat radiating off the hard surfaces. As he reached the summit, he didn't see the vastness of the veld, the herd of zebras mingling with the impala, the shimmering of the day as it blanketed the grasses. He didn't stop. He kept going, placing one foot in front of the other, propelled by the decision to stop the pain. The raven had brought him here so he could end his torment. Each footstep fell on rock, dust, earth and then, with determination, he stepped off the cliff into nothing. He was weightless, free.

He opened his eyes. The cool of evening was drifting in the air. He was sitting at the edge of the precipice. What had happened? Why had he not tumbled through space landing in a broken mass on the rocks below, his breath and pain forever stilled? There was an unfamiliar quiet around his heart. A humming from the rocks permeated his bones, its vibration rumbling through his being, breaking his body into millions of fragments and sending it radiating across the land, down into the soil and up into the heavens. As if led by an unseen hand he rose and walked down from the rocks. The raven appeared again. He followed him to a pond. It was deep and clear with seemingly no bottom. The edge of the pond was soft with leaves deeply decayed into a meld of mud. His feet sank into the ooze on the water's edge, its smell clean and earthy, its feel comforting and soft. Here he knelt. Cupping his hands together, he scooped the water up and over his head. Water cascaded down over his ears, trickling down his back and chest, its coolness awakening and enlivening each cell. He did this again and again, looking to the heavens, asking for guidance.

He paused. A wind stirred and brushed past his face. His eye caught some movement. Something made his heart long for softness, made his body lean into the unknown, beckoning air. He stood up tall and walked forward ever deeper into the water, until his whole body was submerged. He remembered his initiation into manhood, rubbing his body with white clay, racing into the river with the other boys soon to be men, feeling the bite of the cold, watching the clay dissolve into the water. He understood he had not entered into manhood on that day. It was time for him to do so now, but he needed guidance. The community of men had not been able to initiate him.

His mind now turned to rumours he had overheard. Hiding in the dark outside villages, he had heard people talk of a highly revered Sangoma. She was a woman known for a quiet demeanor that belied a fierce ability to cut through meddling demons. It had been a long time since he had acknowledged the Ancestors. It was time to atone for having neglected them. He must ask them to lead him, to show him the way. First, he must make a sacrifice in their honour to ask directions to her doorstep and to find peace in his heart that had been ravaged by years of hatred.

Hlwelo emerged from the water and began walking. He continued to walk as the sun set and the dark gathered. He saw a village over the hills. He made his way to it through the dusk and when all was still inside the enclosure, under the cover of night he slipped inside, quietly found a goat. He slit its throat, and caught the blood in a sack, as best he could. Hlwelo left the village and walked far into the night with the little animal draped across his shoulders, its blood oozing over his skin. Far from the village he stopped to make the sacrificial fire. As he poured the goat's blood into the fire, he offered the animal to the Ancestors, requesting peace for his tormented soul. Then he cooked and ate his fill of its flesh and left the rest to the scavenger animals. He cut strips of the goat's hide to take with him.

He walked through the next day, stopping only to gather some sage in his path. He tied it with a piece of the goat hide and placed it in his sack. He walked on. The raven appeared on the morning of the next day. He followed. The raven flew on ahead and circled three times over a collection of rocks and trees and then disappeared.

When Hlwelo approached the grove, he saw a lone hut. Many sacks of different shapes and sizes were hanging on the branches of the trees. He knew he had arrived at the hut of the Sangoma. He waited until he heard a voice inviting him to enter. Once inside, he bowed in the appropriate respectful greeting. Through the dim light he saw the woman, seated on a large cow skin. Her hair was graying at the temples, her face quiet and unrevealing. He saw many more sacks hanging on the walls of the hut. She gestured for him to sit. He laid at her feet the offering of the sage weed. He looked up and found the Sangoma's eyes on him. His body began to shudder and tremble. He had heard she was powerful but it had never occurred to him that he might fear her. He waited for her to speak, reassuring himself that it was right that he had come, that his reaction must mean that she had the power to expose and banish these overwhelming demons that tormented him.

Mfundi looked at the sack he had offered and heard the cry of the goat. She looked up and held his gaze. Here at last was the face of her assailant. Her body went cold. A wave of numbness spread throughout her limbs, followed by fire erupting in her woman place. She closed her eyes. She felt the wound in her body, her heart racing. Her body jerked repeatedly. He was no longer a phantom that invaded her mind from the dark cracks in her ungraspable shadows. He was here now, in front of her. She saw a vision of Doyenne smiling at her and slowly her body grew quiet; she re-inhabited her arms and legs, feeling the earth warm beneath her. She opened her eyes.

"Why have you come?" she asked.

"I am haunted by demons," he said. "My body and mind are not my own. I wish to be free of the pain."

"Why do you come to me?"

"I have heard your connection to the Ancestors is strong and you have great power to cast out evil. I have appealed to the Ancestors but they do not hear me. I am powerless in the face of this curse that I am under."

Mfundi watched him so wrapped in his own despair that he did not recognize her. She felt sad that so much of his life had been locked in bitterness and sorrow, unable to see anything else of the world that was in front of him.

"Let us throw the bones and hear the Ancestors speak."

Mfundi untied the bulging lion skin pouch from the belt at her waist. She handed the pouch to Hlwelo and told him to hold it with both hands, touching it first to his forehead, then to his heart, and finally to his navel, then to roll the bag between his hands and blow his breath into it. She made him repeat these actions two more times. Then she covered his hands and the pouch with her hands and held them there. Hlwelo felt a tingling in his hands that traveled up his arms and into his head. Mfundi took the pouch, repeated the sequence herself, opened the pouch and threw the contents. The objects from within came spilling out, scattering as if in slow motion: small shells, bone fragments, bird beaks and claws. They came to rest on the cow skin.

"Look to your past," she said. "These demons you carry have been inside you for a long time, since you were a young boy. You have been feeding them with hatred and bitterness ever since. Your heart was locked in anger and these demons joyfully took root in you, happy to flourish on what you fed them, happy to cripple and destroy you. But far beyond their reach is the untouched place inside this little boy before his heart turned cold. He has been lost for a very long time. He is stirring and he wants you to know him. It is the fight between that innocent boy and these demons that causes you so much pain. This is where we must begin."

Mfundi stood, picked up a rock with a deep hollow in its centre and went to the many bags hanging on the walls of her hut. She paused in front of each bag, opening some, moving past others. She put pinches of different herbs and barks into the bowl in the rock. She came to sit in front of Hlwelo, cleared the bones to one side, took another stone and ground the mixture together. She handed the bowl to Hlwelo. She took a lion skin that was hanging from the rafters and covered him with it. As she lit the mixture in the bowl, she told him to breathe in its smoke until the mixture had completely finished burning.

Hlwelo breathed in the sharp, sweet fragrance in the darkness under the skin, seeing only the embers glowing. When it seemed that the embers were about spent, suddenly towering flames appeared and he heard their roar. It was the Great Fire. He heard the screaming of the villagers. He saw himself as a young boy running alongside Mnani. He saw Mnani place his father's lifeless body by the river. He saw the moment this young boy shut his heart. He walked over to his young self in the vision, wanting to touch him somehow but the young boy stood up and passed right through him, expressionless as he walked away. Hlwelo moaned under the lion skin, feeling the weight of the boy's decision to close his heart.

Mfundi saw in her own mind what Hlwelo was seeing in his.

"You have been running your whole life trying to escape. You will never be free if you run. Only when you stop and look into the heart of your running, into the heart of your pain, can you begin to be free. You have bemoaned the colour of your skin, the fate of your mother, the death of your father. You have believed your pain is you. You know this pain well. You must ask what is beyond the pain. This takes courage and strength. Use the powerful forces of your hate and your sense of injustice instead to focus beyond the dark. It will lead you to what you are truly seeking. The strength of your hate is as strong as your ability to step beyond it. Focus. Pull your sight back into the centre of your head. Go inside. Pierce the veil of darkness that you wear. It is what your heart yearns for. Your deepest self knows what lies beyond and it is calling you there. It is what held you rooted on the mountaintop. It is what has brought you to me. Breathe. Go into that still point and when you have found it then follow it."

Hlwelo closed his eyes, pulling his focus back as she had instructed. He went into his hate, felt its familiar heat and the thrill of its power. Suddenly he felt a pull and he lifted up out of the hate and hung suspended…in what? He did not know. As he grew more and more still a blue-white light began to shimmer. This unfamiliar space had no form, no substance. His mind tried to find something to hold on to.

"Let go of your thoughts, your efforts, your need to know. Let the blue light carry you," Mfundi said.

Hlwelo hung suspended with no sense of time or space, only a calm openness. Gradually he felt his limbs again, took a deep breath and removed the lion skin from his head.

"I saw a Great Fire that happened in my village when I was a young boy. I think I understand," he said.

"There is more," Mfundi replied, "but for now it is enough. You must go into the veld. Make a request to the Ancestors that your vision will be clear. Ask to be shown the path into your deepest self where there is access to all wisdom. You will know when to perform another goat sacrifice. Be careful how you choose this goat. Go into the veld and when you have reached your destination, inhale more of this mixture with your head covered as you have done here today. I will follow my own journey and request the same access to where we are all united in the Great Wisdom. The Ancestors will guide you. You will know their directions if you listen. Return here when it is time."

Hlwelo bowed to Mfundi and, taking the small bag of herbs and the skin he set out into the veld. He was tired but determined, knowing that he must find a way to heal this broken boy's heart. He turned his mind to how best to prepare to follow the Sangoma's instructions.

JOURNEYING

Mfundi watched Hlwelo leave. She looked up into the rolling hills and then picked up the contents of the sack, repeated the ritual and threw them again. In the bones she read the clear message from the Ancestors: return to your childhood home to heal yourself and your village. Assure the Chief that the village can be restored to health and abundance.

Her chest contracted with a shot of pain. She didn't want to go back to her village. She didn't want to remember. She didn't want to step on the earth where Doyenne had once played and where Mandla still walked. The pain spread through her back. She bent down and rested her forehead on the earth.

"Please don't ask me to go," she whispered.

She thought she had healed those deep hurts. She wanted the past to be done, to not intrude on her life anymore. She breathed in the damp smell of the dirt as the night descended. She knew she had to go. She lifted her head. She stood up. She set out on her journey.

It had been many years since she had seen her village. As she approached she heard the call of the river. She felt she was Ntombi once again. She walked along the river for a while and sat down. She threw a stone into the centre of the river and watched the ripples. She pondered how every part of creation overlapped, just like these ripples in the river. She saw the inextricable way her life and Hlwelo's had been entwined; not only as young children together innocently, not only with their lives torn asunder by the fire and the assault, but since then, both living in one another's shadow. Each lived with the other invisibly close over their shoulder whispering beyond hearing, until being brought to this intersection in time to have the whisperings finally heard, so a response could finally be made.

Her body doubled over. This is how it was when she stepped back into memory. This is how it was when she let down her guard and the past rose up through the dark corridors of time. This is how it was when her wounding broke through her carefully crafted defenses. Her body buckled in on itself and the heaviness in her chest would begin again. She felt the invisible weight pressing on her, the phantom body insisting its way into hers. She remembered the constriction in her throat, trying to utter a sound, any sound, that might alert someone to the injustice that was being done, alert them to the smothering fear that was suffocating her, alert them to the innocence that was being stolen.

Mfundi bowed her head low until the top of her tight curls touched the dust. "Help me," she uttered softly.

The cage around her heart was cracking. The blood rushed to her head as she remained doubled down to the earth.

"Help me," she whispered again.

She had not known that she had still been so locked up inside. She had thought through all the years of her training she had shed the shackles that held her. But now the ground had fallen away and the extent to which she was still a prisoner revealed itself. She lifted her head. Looking into the air, she saw millions of points of light separating and reconfiguring, new patterns emerging, reality rearranging. Rivers of energy spread throughout her limbs, a prickling presence as light pulsed into untouched pathways, awakening every cell of her being.

She looked around her. All was quiet, save for the small sound of the clear water trickling through the smooth stones at the river's edge. Her eyes scanned the banks. The tree where she had first felt full love for Mandla was still there, rooted and strong. She looked into the water, the outline of worn rocks dissolving as they sloped into the depths, that still held Doyenne's last breath. This river held the shaping of her life. It held her hope, her joy and her sorrow.

She watched the liquid current as it changed, even as it appeared the same. And here she was after all these years, pulled, shaped and changed by the current of events that transformed all she knew, forcing her to let go of any desire to hold on, to have life be different than it was. She had been stripped of everything by fire, by water, by stone, by force and by choice. She entered the cool depth of the river, her breath suspended, her eyes open. As she submerged, the brilliant shafts of light bent toward her through the water. She felt a small hand take hold of hers and she looked into the eyes of her sweet baby. As she ascended through the water, Doyenne grew from her tiny self through the intervening years to a young woman. Together they emerged from the depths coming to float effortlessly, with hands still clasped. The pull of the river now moved them in gentle circles, each occupying the space from which the other had just drifted, mother and daughter moving in and out of each other.

Mfundi opened her eyes. She was sitting by the river, the water trickling through the stones at its edge. She sat for a very long time in silence. Then she got up, gathered some dry brush and built a small fire. She watched the smoke curl upwards and, invoking the Ancestors, began to sing, her voice carrying all the years of her heart's longing and wounding. Her body joined with the song, her dance full and wild.

It was almost dawn when she finally stopped. Her body was spent, the sweat running rivers down her arms, torso and legs. She sat down and began to cry. Throughout the long night she had danced, transported by powers beyond her finite self. Long ago she had let go of any attempt to understand or control the energy that came through her, the innumerable images of fire, sparks, light, the endless sensations of tingling, surges, swoons. The Ancestors held her and carried her. She trusted them, and she trusted herself.

As the sky gathered light, Mfundi looked around her. The fire had been reduced to small puffs of smoke occasionally rising from the bed of fine ash. She carefully dragged her long elegant fingers through the ash and mixed the fine dust with her sweat. Creating a paste, she traced swirls and streaks along the contours of her magnificent face, the proud outline of her firm jaw, the bones encircling her deep eyes, her fierce brow. She followed the slope under her chin, resting for a moment in the hollow at the base of her neck, feeling the rhythmic thud of her heartbeat. She continued down her breastbone, pausing in the centre of her chest feeling the pulsing warmth emanating from it. With her other hand she retrieved more ash from the pit and encircled her breasts with the grey paste. With both hands now she grabbed handfuls of ash and rubbed it vigorously over her belly, then from her thighs down to her feet; more ash now over her buttocks, down the backs of her legs and finally up, crowning her head and tight black curls. She was completely covered, the ash mingling with the colour of her dark skin. In a rush she realized she must look like Hlwelo, his dark skin mixed with the seed of the white man. She drank him in, allowing all his anguish deep into her pores, feeling the pain of his isolation. She breathed in his bitterness, his hatred of all things beautiful. Her heart cracked open with sorrow and tenderness. The violation he had thrust upon her dissolved. Any remnant of anger or hurt melded with the ash. She walked down to the river and slowly, slowly stepped one foot, two feet, knees, thighs, buttocks, woman place, belly, breasts, arms, hollow of neck, head, and finally crown into the waiting water. It enfolded her, washing her clean. All traces of the story she had held from so long ago washed away in the healing waters and floated down toward the vast bottomless ocean, the holder of all mystery.

Mfundi left the river and walked to her childhood village. She waited at the gate until the Chief's son came.

"I seek permission to enter," Mfundi said.

"Wait here, I will bring the Chief," was the reply. He disappeared and returned with the Chief.

"Greetings, Inkosi, have you slept well?"

"Yes, I have slept well," he replied.

He struggled to place who it was standing before him. His heart was full of joy and sorrow at the same time, a full ache in his chest.

"And is it a good day, Inkosi?"

The eyes with such a direct gaze… and the voice, yes, the voice, it was clear and full and rich….he remembered.

"It is a good day," he replied. "It is a very good day. I am happy to see you again, Ntombi, after so much time. Or I should say, Mfundi? Our village has taken great pride in your accomplishment. You are well known and well respected. I am honoured that you have returned."

"Thank you, Inkosi," Mfundi said meeting his gaze with a smile. "You are well?"

"Yes, I am well."

"And Mama Wiyaka, she is well?"

"Mama Wiyaka is well," he said with a smile.

"And, Gosololo? I see her often in the dream time."

"Gosololo has joined the Ancestors," the Chief replied.

"Yes, I had thought perhaps that was why she was visiting me so often now." She paused. "The Ancestors have directed me to come to assure you that opportunity for healing is coming to the village, and peace for those who lost their lives here. You have the opportunity to be a part of that healing. You will know how to help when the time comes."

The Chief's heart lifted and he smiled.

"I am glad you have come, Mfundi. Thank you for your message from the Ancestors."

"If I may, I would like to walk through the village."

"Of course, you are most welcome."

Mfundi bowed her head gently and took her leave of the Chief. She wandered through the village, so changed from the place she had once known. It had grown. Many more huts and homesteads now clustered in the village, but she still knew where she was going. She went to Gogo's burial ground and placed her forehead against the Buffalo Thorn tree, remembering the branch she had taken with her when she set out from the village so long ago.

She wandered through the village. She nodded to the women she passed, some weaving reeds into baskets or bending over the fires, cooking a meal. As she passed hut openings, she saw women grinding corn to flour, their bodies rocking back and forth. She smiled at the old men sitting together throwing pebbles at a ring of stones, or dozing as they straddled a stump, with hands and head resting on a thick stick. She saw children playing the same stick games she remembered from her childhood.

Her heart took an unexpected beat as she saw a young man walking towards her. It was unmistakeable…the way he carried his body, his nose, his cheeks, his eyes… this was Mandla's boy… Mandla and Nombulani's boy… but he was not a boy, he was a young man, clearly well past his initiation time with a body that had filled into a man's, a beautiful young man. He smiled at her as he passed. She turned to look at him just as he turned to look back at her. There was a look of puzzlement on his face. She wanted to reach out and clutch him to her heart, to step through time and return to when she and Mandla were this age and feel the closeness of him again against her skin. Instead she nodded her head and smiled. He smiled, imperceptibly shook his head, and turned to continue on his way.

Mfundi went back to the Chief's hut. She saw Mama Wikaya preparing the fire and said, "Mama Wikaya, I am happy to see you."

Mama Wiyaka looked up. She took a moment, and then she saw through the face so changed with time to the young woman who had left the village long ago. She stood up, opened her arms wide, and encircled Mfundi with a hearty embrace.

"You have made your village very proud. I imagine it must have been a long and difficult journey for you since I last saw you. Now you have become a great healer. It is a testament to your determination and your big heart. I remember well your big heart. And have you, yourself, found healing?"

Mfundi paused, wondering if she would ever find complete healing. She looked around the Chief's homestead and down through the village to the fields outside the gate and thought about the heaviness in her heart when she had left her village. Her heart was infinitely lighter now and when the darkness did encroach on her it didn't stay as long. She was more able to withstand the pain, and she thought perhaps that was what true healing was. She was never going to have a life without pain, no one would, but what mattered was how to be with the pain.

She looked at Mama Wiyaka and said, "Yes, I am able to hold the pain of my past in a way that allows me to love life, even in moments of deep sorrow. I am alive and full with all the moments of joy and sadness."

"My heart smiles knowing that you are well," Mama Wikaya said.

The Chief stepped out of his hut and approached the women.

"We are happy you have returned to your village, Mfundi. You are welcome here always."

"Thank you, Inkosi. Hlalagahle, stay in peace."

Together the Chief and Mama Wikaya said, "Hambagahle, go in peace."

"Thank you," she said and turned to walk through the village back to her life as Mfundi.

HEALING

Hlwelo walked through the veld with the herbs Mfundi had given him, along with instructions to find the place that the Ancestors would choose for him. He was worried that he would not recognize the place. He felt he was being tested and that he would fail, just as he felt that he had failed all his life. Just now, when he was ready to finally embrace something he had been reaching toward for a long time, he was afraid it would be beyond his grasp. He feared he would be doomed to live out his days held by the shadow of his failings. Hlwelo walked out through the low bush for an hour, waiting to feel some instruction from the Ancestors. None came. He looked all around him. He could see nothing in the landscape to indicate a special place. He continued walking, hoping some sign would undeniably declare the spot he should occupy. After another hour, still nothing had showed itself. The light of the day was beginning to change as the sun moved towards its resting place. Hlwelo was starting to panic. He started off at a slow trot hoping to arrive at his unknown destination faster than by walking. Another hour went by. Finally, as the sky was dark, he stopped, exhausted by his efforts. Here it was again, his failure hanging heavy in his heart. He hated this defeated place in himself. He threw back his head, opened his mouth and let out a scream that held all his frustration, all his sense of worthlessness, of hopelessness. He let the bag of herbs from Mfundi drop as he sank to the ground. Eventually he became silent and still. A wind began to blow. It swirled around him picking up the bag of herbs and placing it a few feet in front of him. The wind cleared all the twigs and leaves three feet in all directions around the bag.

As quickly as it had arrived, the wind abruptly subsided. Hlwelo took the animal skin and the flat stone from his sack and entered into the circle. He placed some of the herb and bark mixture on the stone, lit them and covered himself with the skin. He sat inside the enclosure with the smoke rising from the smoldering herbs. Closing his eyes, Hlwelo breathed in deeply. The sweet, fragrant smoke entered far into his chest.

Relaxed, he opened his eyes and watched random patterns burning in the herbs, mesmerized by the changing shapes. His body was pulled into the orange red glow and emerging through the other side of the colours, he found himself standing in the veld.

It was dusk. The light was purples and oranges, with the outline of an escarpment in dark contrast. He saw a solitary figure. Even from this distance he could tell it was a woman seated on a ledge. Her gaze traveled over the drop of land in front of her. She was clearly absorbed in some private world. He approached quietly, not wanting to disturb her, but eager to understand who she was and why he had been brought to her. He seated himself beside her. For a long while she remained silent, motionless. Then she turned towards him. Her face was old, weathered. Her eyes held a kindness that, for some reason, made him feel lonely. He waited for her to speak. She studied him. Her fingers reached out and traced the outline of his face, soft fingers that left a strange sensation in their wake as they traveled over his forehead, cheekbones, broad nose, full lips. She lowered her hand and smiled.

"My son," she said.

Hlwelo's breath caught in his chest. As he looked into her eyes her face changed into that of a beautiful young woman whose eyes were filled with sadness and pain. Her face was covered in sweat. He saw her body lying on a reed mat holding a bloody mottled newborn. Her eyes filled with tears.

"I'm sorry," she said. "I'm sorry I had to leave you. The Ancestors called me. It broke my heart. Even though you were sent to me through much pain, I loved you for that brief moment I held you, and I have loved you ever since. I felt so helpless as I watched you over the years, lashing out and stumbling along your way. I knew the hurt and sorrow your heart held, and watched as you chose to channel it all into a burning rage against everything. I could not reach through that thick barrier that encased your heart. I have been with you always, calling your name, honouring the goodness I knew was hidden inside you, praying that you would one day find the key to unlock your prison of bitterness. I was there at the precipice when you chose to end your life. Somewhere you heard my call to stay. My son, my beautiful, tortured son. The Gods have finally answered my prayers and you can now hear me. Allow your heart to break open to the love that is everywhere."

Hlwelo felt a sharp pain in his chest as if a stake was being driven deep into him. The pain was unbearable. All the loss and loneliness he had fought off flooded through every crack and crevice of his being.

"It is too much," he cried out. "It will kill me." He gasped for breath as if he was drowning.

"Help me," he cried.

His mother's arms were around him, cradling him, rocking him back and forth. A soft humming came from her lips as his body shook with sobs. His mother's love that had been denied him all these years now surrounded him – solid, steady, holding him fast until his tears eventually began to subside. His breathing calmed and he felt himself melt into her, their bodies the same body. In complete comfort he slipped into sleep.

When he woke he was wrapped snugly in the animal skin. Day was dawning. Hlwelo sat for a long time remembering the vision of his mother. He looked over the veld, seeing the open expanse and the subtle colours that blended into one another. He lit another batch of herbs, covered his head with the animal skin, breathed in the smoke and closed his eyes.

When he opened them again he found himself standing in the middle of a river. Facing him was a young woman with a girlish face. Her skin was pale, her eyes a deep green. She had a broad flat nose and full lips. Her hair was close to her scalp in the short tight curls of the women of his childhood village. She smiled at him even as her eyes were filling with tears. She looked familiar but he didn't know her.

"Who are you?" Hlwelo asked.

"You don't know me because you never knew of me. I died many years ago. Even though my life on the earth was short, I have continued to grow on the other side. I have followed you for many years, hoping that one day you would have the sight to see me."

Hlwelo looked at this beautiful young woman. He didn't understand. How did she know him?

"Look at my eyes", she said.

Hlwelo felt a pang in his heart. He thought of his childhood village and the young girl he had loved and hated.

"Look at my skin," she said. It was the same creamy colour as his own. His mind rebelled at the possibility.

"It cannot be," he said.

"Yes," she said softly, "I am your daughter. You never knew me because you ran. You ran that night after you played your part in my creation. I was born to an absent father and a broken mother. She endured humiliation and isolation because of me, but she loved me with a fierceness that eventually opened others to love me, in spite of my dark beginnings. Your actions that night plunged her into a melting fire of despair that would remold her. I was called by the Ancestors to leave her early to stoke that fire, so that she would become strong enough to take on her life's calling. I have waited for this day. My heart is glad that you can now know me."

Hlwelo stared, his mind numb. How could he never have known somewhere deep inside that he had created a child? How would his life have been different if he had stayed that night and not run away? But he had to run. There was no way he could stay after what he had done. There was no way that Ntombi could have forgiven him. She would have despised the sight of him. She would never have allowed him to love her. He had to run. It was his inability to run any further that allowed him to finally see his daughter.

"What is your name?" Hlwelo asked.

"Doyenne," she replied.

Hlwelo timidly moved through the water towards her. "May I hold you?"

She smiled, "I have waited all these years for my father's arms."

He tentatively put his arms around her thin body. The water began to swirl until it encircled them both, his body dissolving into hers, hers into his. He felt all the loneliness and longing for love he had carried for so long drain out of him, merging with the water. Here was this lovely young woman bearing him no anger, no bitterness. How many years had she lived? What had her life been? How did she die? How could he make up for what he had done? He closed his eyes allowing Doyenne's embrace to seep into his bones.

When he opened his eyes, he found himself lying on the dark earth, huddled in the fetal position, alone. He pulled the animal skin close around him and stayed there motionless, eventually falling into a dreamless sleep.

Hlwelo woke to the sound of the umzwilili birds. The increasing light of the beginning day revealed a peaceful landscape. For the first time he could see the colours of the changing sky. He could feel its beauty resounding deep inside him. In the past, each dawning day had released him from his tortured dreams only to reconnect him with his despair. But now he was different. He could still feel the closeness of his mother and his child. All through his lonely wanderings they had been at his side, but his hatred of the world, and of himself, had hidden them from his view. Now he could see them clearly, and feel their hearts beating in rhythm with his own. He sat for a while longer watching a small herd of impala as they grazed quietly, their tails lazily swatting away tiny insects.

Hlwelo sat with the memory of the visitations. How he longed to see each of them again. He felt a renewed sense of the loss of his mother. He almost wished he had not seen her. The lifetime of her absence felt even more painful, now that he had seen her flawless face and had heard her gentle voice. And if only he had known his daughter had existed, she might have saved him from his life of lonely wandering. He looked to where she had risen in water, now seeing only grassland and open spaces. There had been magic in the water. She was the magic. He must remember her words and allow them to seep into every crease and crevice of his being. He must take her and his mother deep into his chest, hold them within and draw from their strength and love. They were a gift from the Ancestors sent to deliver him from his dark torture. He would return to the Sangoma, thank her and tell her of the visions held in the herbs, for he now felt healed.

After days of fasting and the intensity of the visions, Hlwelo felt the grumblings of hunger. It was a curiously happy feeling. Having spent so many years not really tasting or enjoying anything he ate, he now was impatient to eat. He gathered his things and set off in the direction of Mfundi's hut. When he came to the shores of the river, he found some berries. They were perfectly formed, each berry a tapestry of symmetrical design, delicate to the touch, with a gentle fragrance. He took his time rolling one carefully between his fingers, admiring it from every angle. He had no vengeful thoughts of the white man, only wonder at such a perfect creation held in hand. He closed his eyes directing the ripe fruit into his mouth, closed his teeth over the berry and slowly bit down releasing the intense juice. The taste was exquisite. He grinned like a young boy. He picked more berries, crammed more into his mouth, and squished them in his hands watching the red nectar drip through his fingers. He rubbed them

over his arms and laughed with delight. He plunged into the river feeling
the shock of the cool water. This was the river of his childhood, the river
where he met his daughter, the river of the Sangoma, the life-giving river
that cleansed and initiated him. He emerged refreshed, glistening in the
mid-morning sun. He gathered more berries to bring to Mfundi, placing
them carefully in the sack that had held the herbs. He was eager to relay
his experiences of the past few days. He traveled throughout the day,
content knowing that tomorrow he would find himself once again in the
reassuring presence of Mfundi.

He walked in the direction of the Sangoma's hut but after a short
time something pulled him to turn around and go in the opposite
direction. The more he resisted the more his legs began to feel like heavy
rocks and his breathing grew difficult. He turned to look towards the
sun lowering in the sky. He thought he could make out something in
the distance and as he gazed out at the horizon, his body felt a surge of
lightness. But he wanted to get to Mfundi before dark and turned again
to face the direction of her hut. Again he felt the heaviness in his body
that made it difficult for him to continue. He turned once more toward
the setting sun and he became mesmerized. Something inside him fell
away and the light on the horizon began to glow, not with the usual
colours of a savannah sunset but with a metallic sheen. Hlwelo heard a
rushing sound in his ears. A shape emerged on the horizon. It was the
figure of a fierce Mswembe warrior coming towards him, wearing a lion
tooth and claw necklace with a leopard skin encircling his shoulders, the
ritual adornments of royalty. The warrior glared at Hlwelo and raised
his hand. It was missing a finger. He pointed at him and then swung his
arm to point in the direction of the setting sun. It was the direction of
his childhood village. Hlwelo understood. He was afraid, knowing there
was more to come. He took one step and then another, moving towards
his past with a heavy dread in his heart. He was ready to surrender to
what the Ancestors would next reveal to him. His fear was strong but his
determination was stronger.

THE VILLAGE

Lightning flickered distant across the veld, so far and so faint it might not have actually happened at all. It could have just been an illusion that The Chief wanted to see, so in need of rain was his village. He sighed, his eyes scanning the distance. Nothing. No rolling thunder, no more flashing light. His heart was sad. His people were hungry, livestock were dying, crops were sparse and tough. The drought extended far and wide. Many other villages were also suffering. A curse had descended on the land and he was at a loss as to how to lead his people through it.

The Chief looked again to the horizon – nothing – only the dark silhouette of the far mountains. The curse would not be lifted tonight. No rain would come tonight. He sighed again and he felt he must atone in some way before the heavens would open and bless the earth with its sweet nectar, but what form that atonement would take, he had no idea.

Hlwelo saw the outline of the village in the distance. He knew he must make this journey back, to stand again where it had all begun. He stumbled and fell. A tiny stone ground a sharp point into his knee. Its sting sent a chill through his body. His stomach began to lurch. There was too much history. He did not want to remember or to feel any of it. He had spent many years running from it, but he knew he must return.

He got up and approached the village. As was proper, he waited at the rough wooden gate at the entrance of the muzi. Eventually a tall young man came. Hlwelo would have recognized the features of the Chief in this young face, even without knowing it would be one of the Chief's sons who would come, as was the custom. The sons of the Chief must know who comes and goes from the village, and be at hand when the Chief receives visitors. Then when they take over after the Chief's death, they are already familiar with the business and the temperament of those whose visits they will receive.

"I seek permission to enter," Hlwelo said.

"Wait here, I will bring the Chief," was the reply.

The Chief approached, a loincloth of white cowhide covering his manhood, a wildebeest tail woven on the end of a carved stick in his left hand.

"Greetings, Inkosi, have you slept well?" "Yes, I have slept well," he replied.

"And is it a good day, Chief?"

"It is a good day," he replied.

"I have brought some berries," said Hlwelo bowing to the Chief in respect and handing them to the Chief's son. "May I enter?"

The Chief paused for a moment, and then said, "You may enter."

"*Ngiyabonga*," Hlwelo said bowing his head again.

The gate was opened and Hlwelo followed the Chief to his hut situated at the top of the muzi. The Chief sat on a smoothed stump and gestured Hlwelo to take one opposite him.

As was the custom, the Chief's first wife brought the calabash, their symbol of friendship and hospitality, filled with a newly fermented batch of beer. After stirring the brew, Mama Wikaya filled the small serving spoon and poured the liquid over the ground beside the Chief, inviting the Ancestors to join the gathering and to drink with them. Then she took a small taste, nodded her head and passed the container with the scoop to her husband. The Chief tasted the earthy liquid and nodded to her. She withdrew to her hut.

The Chief offered some to Hlwelo who received the spoon with both hands, his head bowed. When they had both drunk from the gourd the Chief spoke.

"I know who you are. Your skin announces you."

The pulse in the Chief's temple flashed in the sun with each strong beat.

"It has been many rains since you have been in our village. Why have you come back?"

"I am under the guidance of the Sangoma, Mfundi, to try to heal a sickness that I have carried deep in my heart since I was a young boy, a bitterness and fear that have made me hate and do harm. I wish to be free from these demons I carry inside. She has told me to listen to the Ancestors and I believe they have instructed me to come here. If you will allow it, I wish to sit inside the isibaya, to feel the centre of my boyhood village."

The Chief looked at Hlwelo knowing well his story, for it had been clear to everyone why Hlwelo had disappeared once Ntombi had her baby. As Chief, it was his calling to protect his people and he still felt the burden of having failed to protect young Ntombi. He could see the pain in this man's eyes, in the lines of anguish that had carved pathways on his face, in the bend of his body. Part of him wanted to punish this man, whip him and stake him on top of an anthill to watch with satisfaction as the ants burrowed deep into his open wounds. He closed his eyes and silently whispered a call to the Ancestors for guidance. He opened his eyes and saw before him a man seeking forgiveness, a man who had lived his life in self- imposed banishment.

"You may go to the isibaya," he said.

Hlwelo bowed, picked up his skin of water and slowly walked from the Chief's presence. When he was in the centre of the village he stood still and looked all around him. It looked much the same as it had when he was a boy, even though all the huts now standing were not the ones he had seen consumed by fire. They were replacements, built in the same tradition of construction. He felt their familiarity. People bustled about as though there had been no painful history in this place, while all Hlwelo could think of was the terrible loss of his father and how he had chosen to close his heart, and turn away from this village and anything that would remind him of his loneliness and pain. Young children, their eyes wide with disbelief, stopped their play as they saw him, never having seen one whose features resembled theirs so closely but whose skin seemed to bleed the colour of the moon.

Hlwelo looked up the gentle slope of the hill to the circle of fence where the animals would return in the evening. He remembered his father telling him how interdependent the village and the animals were.

"We feed the animals," he would say, "rain washes their manure down from the isibaya into the fields to fertilize the crops. When the animals die, their bodies still continue to give gifts: food to eat, hides for clothes and blankets, skins to cover carved drums to make music, sinews for sewing. The animals remain with us long after their blood has stopped flowing. We must honour them with respect, thanking them for what they give us through their life and again through their death."

Hlwelo looked down through the opening of the village to the fields of corn and squash. He remembered back to the time of his childhood when he still had hope for happiness. He swallowed hard remembering Ntombi's innocent laughter as she would skip through the fields with her grandmother.

He waited until the animals had been brought in and the gate of the village secured. He made his way into the isibaya. He looked through the wooden stakes. The villagers were at their huts settling themselves down with the settling of the day. He saw the fire pit in the centre of the village and the fire keeper preparing for the night, arranging the wood, poking the fire and finally seating himself to face the gate to see any intruders who might try to enter the village under the cover of dark.

Hlwelo felt the pang of the memory of that horrific night from his childhood, and the weight of the blame he had placed on Dinzane. Now here he sat, pulled by some unknown force to his childhood village. He waited. The Chief had allowed him entrance to his isibaya. He felt his salvation depended on this one night. What if there were no visitations? What if the Ancestors chose to abandon him now?

As the warmth of the day was replaced by the cool of the evening, he moved closer to the cows seeking the heat from their breath and their skin. He pressed his head into the flank of the proud white bull, the Chief's prized animal. He moved his chest flat against the sturdy beast and felt the pulse of its life. He breathed in the musty smell of sweat, hide and dung. He lifted his head and looked toward the Buffalo Thorn tree where the Ancestors dwelled. He moved to the tree and settled himself at its base, pressing his back against its trunk. Soon his eyes drooped and he drifted into a dreamlike state.

The gate to the isibaya opened and a figure stepped through. Hlwelo's eyes widened and he trembled at the sight. It was Dinzane, burned almost beyond recognition.

"No," he prayed, "no, please do not bring him to me."

But on he came until he stood directly before him. Dinzane's eyes were hollow, his flesh raw and burned. Hlwelo shuddered. Dinzane moved closer and sat down, a hair's breadth distance between them. Hlwelo tried to turn away, but his body would not move. His eyes could not look anywhere but into the deep vacant sockets of the spectre in front of him. As Hlwelo remembered all his years of hatred, all the curses he had uttered, the skin on Dinzane's body sizzled and snapped, the stench of burning flesh overpowering, waves of nausea engulfing Hlwelo. He couldn't breathe, his fear rising with the bile in his throat. The skin of the phantom dropped in patches on the earth, bones charred and splintered poked through. Hlwelo gagged, his body taut and shivering. From the depths of his chest he felt a crack, heard the sound of bone shattering. Amid the terror and agony he heard his own small voice.

"I'm sorry", he wept quietly, "I'm sorry, I'm sorry."

His body rocked. Each time he uttered the same words, the horror in front of him changed. Piece by piece, Dinzane's body reconstructed, became whole, strong and shining. The two men sat across from each other, locked in a hypnotic gaze. Dinzane's eyes were filled with gentleness and calm. Bit by bit Hlwelo's body relaxed. A light rose from Dinzane's navel, traveling up his body through his head and out his eyes, into Hlwelo's eyes where it traveled down through his body, out his navel and across to Dinzane. And so they sat with the continuous circuit flowing unbroken until the moon had risen high. Gradually the thread of light between them diminished and dissolved.

"Thank you," Dinzane said.

The gate opened and Nyongo came forward and sat on the ground beside Dinzane. Hlwelo extended his hand to touch his father, but his hand moved through the apparition while a tingling spread over his skin and into his bones. Nyongo nodded to his son.

"I have been waiting a long time to see you well, my son. It is with great gladness in my heart that I can now come and be here with you alongside Dinzane, who has also been holding you in his heart waiting for this moment. You have never been alone, although you could not see us. Your heart was too tight. There is more to come on this journey. You have come a very long way and now you know you do not walk your path alone. This is the place of your birth, the place of my death. Sit here under the Buffalo Thorn tree and wait. The spirits who dwell here will direct you."

Nyongo and Dinzane rose.

"*Hlalagahle*, stay well," Dinzane said. The two men turned and walked through the animals, dissolving into the night.

Hlwelo rolled to his side and, cupping his head in his hands, slipped into the dreamless sleep of the found and the forgiven.

Hlwelo woke while it was still dark. Feeling well rested, he intended to walk through the village, wait until the Chief was up, thank him and return to Mfundi. Instead, he waited as his father had instructed, listening to the gentle breathing of the animals, smelling the strength of the earth. Eventually he drifted back to sleep and the dreamtime took him. He was in the distant village isibaya where, under the cover of night, he had stolen in and killed a goat as a sacrifice to the Ancestors. Through the darkness of the dream the goat looked up at him and spoke.

"How did you kill me?"

Hlwelo woke with a start, the words of the goat ringing in his head, "How did you kill me?" the goat had asked. Hlwelo sat, consumed by the memory of his dream. He remembered well the night when he had easily slipped into the village. The moon was high, the village silent. He was a ghost floating past the sleeping dogs, making his way to the isibaya. The animals stirred and shifted uneasily, but none cried out declaring his presence. His knife was quick and decisive. The goat was dead before its warm body crumpled to the dirt. Hlwelo collected the red life spilling from its gaping throat into his leather pouch. He slung the limp body across the back of his neck, its blood running across his shoulders and down his back and, as invisible as before, slipped out the gate into the veld.

He traveled until he knew the smell of roasting flesh would not reach the village. He built the fire and trickled blood from the dead animal slowly into the belly of the flames, imploring the Ancestors to release him from his torment. Having made the sacrifice and his fervent prayer, he set about skinning the small beast, skewering pieces of flesh and rotating them at the end of a long stick above the fire. The smell was intoxicating. He had not eaten meat for a long time and eagerly anticipated the gamey taste. He lifted the charred meat to his lips, its heat singeing his lips and tongue. Angrily he cursed the goat, dabbing at his injured lips with his fingers.

So now the goat had come to haunt him in his dreams. "How did you kill me?" What was the meaning of this question? He went over it again in his mind. He did what is required when making a request of the Ancestors... sacrificing a goat, slitting its throat, collecting its blood and offering it up in fire along with the prayer. It had worked for others. It had not worked for him. He had still been plagued by desperation. And why did this goat pose such a question? He closed his eyes and went over it again in his mind...slipping into the village, entering the isibaya. This time the moon grew bigger, brighter, descending in the night sky to hang just above the isibaya, shedding a light that made it neither night nor day. He saw every detail in the isibaya, the piles of manure mixed with straw, the massive bulk of the cows, the flicking of their tails, the musky smell from their snorting nostrils, the goats huddled together in a separate enclosure to one side. He pulled out his knife as he approached the goats, selecting the one with the black and white patches. Just before he was about to plunge his knife into its throat, his arm froze unable to move. The goat looked up at him, a look in its eyes of terror and warning.

In those suspended moments, Hlwelo saw the goat read its fate as it stared into his own dispassionate eyes. There would be no words of thanks for its life and the gifts that that life had given. There would be no commending its spirit to the Gods to be rewarded for having served man well. It would be destined to drift for eternity with no place for its spirit to rest. This goat also knew that not only its own spirit would be left adrift but that the act of this man would not relieve him of his agony, but would only plunge him deeper into misery. His would be a useless death.

Hlwelo now saw all this and he wept for what he had not seen in this animal's eyes, for the disrespect he had shown the village by killing part of their life, for the disrepect he had shown the animal by not honouring its life and death. He understood now why Mfundi had instructed him to make another goat sacrifice.

With the day now advancing, Hlwelo made his way once again to the Chief's hut.

"Sawubona, Inkosi."

"Sawubona," the Chief responded. "Have you slept well, Inkosi?"

"I have slept well," the Chief replied

"And is it a good day?" Hlwelo asked.

"It believe it is a good day," the Chief replied.

"I thank you for allowing me this night in the isibaya. I have another request to ask of you, Great Inkosi."

The Chief was silent, wary of this man who had brought so much suffering to his village. "What is your request?"

"I ask your permission to sacrifice one of your goats. I know I have no right. I ran away from this village a long time ago, after causing great harm. I have tried in my way to ask the Ancestors to release me from my suffering, but I have done so with only the thought of my own release.

I ask you now to allow me to perform ritual again. This time with my deepest desire to apologize for the hurt I brought to this village, the shame I brought to Ntombi and to apologize for the theft and killing of a goat from a distant village and my disregard for its life and service."

The Chief weighed the impact that losing a goat would have on his people. The drought had made all forms of food extremely precious. He also remembered the last time Hlwelo had come to him with the request to sacrifice an ox to honour his father, and his refusal to grant that wish. He knew that refusal had contributed to the dark events that unfolded. Even though the village had successfully rebuilt itself from the ashes of the Great Fire, an unresolved heaviness hung over his people. The Chief closed his eyes and waited. He heard the sound of children laughing and smelled the mealy meal coming from his First Wife's hut. He continued to wait. And then he saw the eyes of the goat, the calm, piercing gaze of one who knows his life is in service. He opened his eyes and looked at Hlwelo.

"I grant your request," he said.

Hlwelo bowed low knowing the weight of what the Chief had granted.

RETURN

When Hlwelo returned to Mfundi's hut she was waiting for him.

"I have prepared some food for you. Eat now and rest. I am going up into the hills and when I return I will hear what you have to tell me."

Hlwelo bowed his head and thanked her. He ate the food with deep appreciation. When he was finished a great fatigue came over him. He lay on the ground, rolled to his side, and using his arm to cradle his head, went to sleep.

Mfundi made her way to the place up the hill where she often sat. By the time she arrived, the day was beginning to wane. At the foot of an acacia tree she found a familiar comfortable position. Deepening and slowing her breathing she half-closed her eyes, softening her gaze allowing her vision to blur slightly. She called on the Ancestors, asking once again for their counsel.

"The moment has come," they said. "He is ready. You are ready. The years of holding are done for you both. The fruit of your actions has ripened. The sorrows from the past may now release into the earth and dissolve back into the Mother. Sit for a while and strengthen your being with our presence. Then go to him and reveal yourself."

Mfundi sat, unmoving, until the sun had set and the moon had begun to rise. Feeling ready and deeply connected to the earth she made her way back to her hut.

After his sleep, Hlwelo had made a fire and was awaiting her return, anxious to recount what he had experienced during his time away.

Mfundi smiled as he recounted the visitations. She had never known Hlwelo's mother in life but had been visited by her from the spirit world many times. She felt lovingly bonded to this woman who had endured such a similar fate as her own. She had witnessed Jabulile's deep sadness at the path of revenge and hatred her son had chosen. She knew Jabulile's spirit to be joyous now that Hlwelo had softened his heart enough to finally see her, after being inaccessible to him yet by his side for so many years.

When Hlwelo began to speak of Doyenne, Mfundi's heart constricted, then filled with a tender love for her carefree child who had been taken so young, and for the beautiful spirit she was becoming as she continued to grow with the Ancestors. Mfundi had felt the healing of her father's spirit body inside her own skin before Hlwelo said anything of his encounter with Dinzane. And Mfundi remembered Nyongo from her childhood as an infinitely kind and gentle man. She had felt the loss of him keenly after the fire, adding weight to the loss of her own family.

When Hlwelo was finished she asked, "Do you know who I am?"

Hlwelo looked at her, puzzled by the question, then answered.

"Yebo, you are a well respected Sangoma, one of the most revered in the land. Many sing of you."

"You have done as the Ancestors have instructed through me and you have seen deep into your pain. You have followed your visions even when you were afraid. The Ancestors are pleased with you. Now they are telling me to have you look, look closely, look with your eyes half-closed, look at me. Pull your eyes back into the middle of your head and see me beyond what you see. Slow your breathing. Go inside your body and pull your eyes in."

Hlwelo slowed his breathing and could feel his limbs release and his body expand. He recognized the sensation in his body signaling that he would be transported within a vision. He had been through this before and knew that whatever he would encounter would be difficult, but if he could stay with it, it would lead to a revelation that freed him in some way. He released into the pull of the unseen vision. As he began to enter in, his body froze, arched, he fought for air. He started to look away from her.

"Do not take your eyes off me," she said.

"I am afraid with a fear I have never known."

"Stay with me, stay with my eyes," she commanded.

His mind began to reel. He was spinning, falling down a dark bottomless well. He landed with a thud. It was dark. He heard soft breathing close by him. He looked around. All he could make out was the outline of an opening to a hut. He saw a shadow cross the threshold. He heard the soft breathing halt. His body tensed with a sense of foreboding. He wanted to run, to leave this place, but he was frozen in his spot unable to move or cry out a warning. He knew something was coming. He wanted to stop it, but stop what? What was about to unfold that he feared?

"Tell me what you see and feel," Mfundi said.

"I am in a hut in the night. Someone has just entered and someone is already inside. I feel a huge weight on my chest and my throat is burning."

Hlwelo heard a low menacing sound like a rabid animal about to attack. The air in the hut began to glow and he could see a young man's figure crouching over a young maiden's body, his hand firmly clasped over her mouth. He heard the low guttural laugh. His bowels flinched with the recognition of himself as a young man and the memory of his vengeful and bitter attack on Ntombi. He tried desperately to pull himself out of the vision.

"Stay where you are, keep breathing," Mfundi said sternly.

Hlwelo could see Ntombi's face contorted with fear. His body was awash with conflicting sensations. It was as if he had entered his young man's body, feeling a burning surge of powerful rage, but he had also entered her body feeling her insides ripping apart with a searing rawness that reverberated deep in his belly. Then he was back in his young man's body again and he stared into Ntombi's eyes. He saw the young girl he had loved as a small child with her laughing eyes. As a young boy, he had loved her with her curious eyes. As a young man, he had desired and hated her with her innocent, sorrowful eyes. He held her gaze as he moved deeper into an opening abyss. And then the eyes became that of the Sangoma. He was staring into the eyes of Mfundi. He was back in her hut surrounded by herbs and bark, beads and drums. He wanted to look away.

"Stay with my eyes," she said and her voice pulled him. He saw and he knew. This was his childhood friend. She was the one he had ripped apart in his need to be free of his unbearable grief. He started to wail.

"Now you know who I am."

"No, it cannot be. This is why the demons have been torturing me. They have brought me to you to punish me."

He started to turn away.

"Look at me," she said, "I am here. Yes, your pain and rage wounded me, but I survived. We both lost much that was consumed in the fire, and our grief set us on a course to bring us to this moment. You were one of the heavy gifts from the Ancestors to lead me to them. And my heart is grateful. There were many years I did not understand and I railed against you and against life. I had lost so much: my family, my innocence, my child, and when Gogo was dying I wanted to give up. But the Ancestors would not allow it. They showed me it was all part of the path to lead me through my years of training. They showed me how to turn my losses into strength. I was rebuilt. And I have been waiting for you. They told me you would come and your coming would free us both. "

Hlwelo stared at her, awed by her radiance. He watched as rainbows of light flickered around her. He saw she was strong and whole. He knew she was powerful. He had not destroyed her. He understood how inseparable they had been through all these distant years. He understood that he had to find her so they could both be free. The weight of his guilt seeped from his head down through his blood, and melted into the earth.

He reached for her, his hand slow and tentative, his fingers moving through the endless space between them. Her hand also reached through the space until the pads of their fingertips connected. The last whispers of pain fell.

Hlwelo lowered his hand. Tears glistened against his pale skin. Here was this unbroken woman in front of him. He had tried to rob her of her goodness. He wept for the hurt he had caused, unable now in his freedom to comprehend his former prison. He thought of the white man and agonized that they both had committed the same vile act.

Could it be that the white man also had a tortured soul that had driven him to destroy any goodness in his path? His heart wept for this man he had spent his lifetime cursing. Hlwelo sent a prayer up to his Soul, asking for forgiveness even as he so forgave. All the heaviness of his heart lifted, unencumbered by his former hatred. He felt weightless, suspended above the earth, able to move freely without restriction in a sea of luminescence. He bowed his head low until it touched the ground at Mfundi's feet, his soul laid bare, stripped of its former ignorance.

Mfundi placed her hands on his head, the warmth from her palms seeping into his scalp. She lifted his head up and smiled. She lit the bundle of sage and, with its fragrant smoke rising to the Ancestors, traced it first around the outline of Hlwelo's body and then around her own, its haze penetrating and connecting them both.

He saw memories from his past rising up and dissolving in front of him. There was no reaction, no fear, no grief, no hate. Over and over, events that had haunted him throughout the years passed through his body of luminescence. He just watched them come and go, an endless stream with no twisted agony, no despair. And each time one arose, it was gone like a bubble in a stream that pops with only the slightest sound. He had no body but was all body. He had no breath but was all breath. He hung in the midst of infinite vastness, no thought, no pain, no self, just endless expansion…utter peace, unshakeable.

"All things arise and pass away, are born and die… people, animals, flowers, crops, villages," she said. "It is the natural law. Wanting it to be otherwise is the cause of all suffering. And, within this series of loss, is endless life, infinite energy found everywhere… the flow of a river, the bursting of a bud, daily miracles of blood and bones…the Great Mystery. Your life's work now is this…to return again and again to this still place that holds everything and nothing until you come to know it so well that it is with you every moment, awake or asleep. Then you will truly be free. With this freedom, your heart will be filled with love. Those who yearn through their pain, as you have, will recognize you. You have been chosen. Through the experience of your own suffering, you can now help them to see beyond their suffering, to find peace beyond the tortured mind. You can help them find freedom. Go now and walk softly on the earth. *Ubuntu,* I cannot be free without you, no one can."

RAIN

The Chief woke and stepped out of his hut to see the sky swollen with rain clouds. As the village began the daily bustle, there was an air of excited expectancy. The rains were coming. Everyone could feel it. It was as if the earth itself rejoiced. Slowly the drops began to fall.

Every pore of land and beast and man opened to receive it. The clouds shifted, darkened, bringing more rain, falling heavily now, increasing in fury until it thundered down. Fingers of rain spread through the powdery orange earth mending the blistered cracks. On and on it poured, the thread of the stream widening, moving, flowing once again. The sweet rains would bring berries back to the bushes, growth back to the crops, flesh back to the cattle, and joy back into their bones. The Gods had finally been appeased and chose to smile again, raining down the juice of life.

The Chief stood outside, his face turned to the sky, each splash against his cheek a welcome relief.

CHARACTER GUIDE

WITH PRONUNCIATION

Ntombi (*N-tom-bee*), daughter of Lindiwe and Dinzane (full name: Bisisiwe Thabisile Lungile)
Lindiwe (*Lin-dee-way*), mother of Ntombi
Dinzane (*Din-zah-nay*), father of Ntombi
Gogo / Nomalanga (*Noma-lang-ga*), grandmother of Ntombi, mother of Lindiwe

Jabulile (*Jabu-lee-lay*), mother of Hlwelo
Nyongo (*Nyong-go*), husband of Jabulile
Hlwelo (*Hl-way-lo*), Sinhawukele, son of Jabulile and the white man

Gosololo (*Go-so-low-low*), friend of Gogo
Mandla (*Mand-la*), Ntombi's love
Nombulani (*Nom-boo-la-knee*), Mandla's wife

Doyenne (*Doy-en-eh*), daughter of Ntombi and Hlwelo
Mwele (*M-way-lay*), one of the village children, a bully

Mfundi (*M-fun-dee*), Ntombi's Sangoma name, means: student, disciple, scholar

Wandisiwe (*Wan-dee-see-way*), Ntombi's Sangoma teacher
The Chief, Chief of the Village
Mama Wikaya (*Wick-eye-ya*), the chief's first and favourite wife
Themba (*Tem-ba*), midwife
Msama (*M-sa-ma*), midwife
Mnani (*M-nah-nee*), a villager
Thandi (*Tan-dee*), village girl, friend of Ntombi
Phumzile (*Pum-zee-lay*), village girl, friend of Ntombi

Cebesile (*Say-bay-see-lay*), village girl, friend of Ntombi

Msueta (*M-sweat-ah*), a woman of the village

Nyela (*N-yea-lah*), a woman of the village

Bongani (*Bong-ga-nee*), Nombulani's father

Kalazone (*Kala-zon-nay*), name of Nombulani's favourite cow, meaning "cry but the tears will eventually dry up; for although things may be going badly now, all will be rectified."

Bhekabantu (*Beck-a-ban-too*), the man who performs circumcisions

Nomkhubulwane (*Nom-koo-bull-wah-nee*), Goddess of Rain, Nature, Fertility

Unkulunkulu (*Un-koo-lun-koo-loo*), the Greatest of all the Ancestors

Shoshani (*Sho-sha-nee*), Sangoma near the Chief's village

Sandiwe (*San-dee-way*), older son of Lindiwe and Dinzane

Bonisiwe (*Boni-see-way*), daughter of Lindiwe and Dinzane

Lwazi (*Lwa-zee*), younger son of Lindiwe and Dinzane

GLOSSARY

Acacia Tree, flat crowned thorn tree, deciduous tree found in Africa, Umsasane

Amadlozi, ancestor, ancestral spirit

Amasi, curdled milk

Assegai, sharp knife used for many things including circumcision

Biltong, dried meat

Buffalo Thorn Tree, a tree where good Ancestral spirits dwell, Umlahlankosi

Emsamo, altar, area in a hut to honour an Ancestor

Gogo, grandmother

Hambagahle, go smoothly, go well, go in peace

Hau!, expression of astonishment, surprise, approval

Hlalagahle, stay well, stay in peace

Igugu, dear

Imbeleko, naming ritual of a new child

Incwadi/themba, a beaded message usually a love letter from a girl to a boy asking to be his girlfriend

Induna, lower-order chief, headman

Ingoyama, lion

Inhlanhla, good luck

Inhlovu, elephant

Inkezo, calabash, gourd

Inkosi, an important chief

Isasa elihle, good morning

Isibaya, enclosure where the livestock is kept at the centre of the village, cattle byre

Isivivane, large pile of stones made by travelers where respect is paid to local spirits to ensure a successfully completed journey

Kopje, a small hill in a generally flat area

Lidloti tree, a tree associated with the Ancestors, believed to hold special powers

Libola/Ilobolo, price paid for a bride, usually 6-12 cows depending on the worth of the woman and the rank of her family

Mealie meal, (uphuthu) mush made from ground corn usually eaten at breakfast

Mswembe, name of the tribe

Muti/umuti, medicine

Muzi/umuzi, village; cluster of dwellings, home to a married man and his family

Ngiyabonga, thank you

Ngiyezwa, I understand

Ntombi, little girl

Sanibonani, good morning to more than one person

Sawubona, I see you; good day, hello, good morning to one person

Tamboti, a medium size deciduous tree, the wood of which has two tones, one a blond colour and the other a reddish brown

Thandiwe, loved

Tokoloshe, demon

Ubaba, father

Ubuntu, we are all men/women together and we must take care of each other; no one can be free until all are free; I cannot be free without you; I am what I am because of who we all are; we are one, we are kind, we are together; communal responsibility; it takes a village to raise a child

Ululations, a high pitched sound made by the women in appreciation and celebration of something

Umama, mother

Umlahlankosi, buffalo thorn tree where good ancestral spirits dwell

Umnumzane, undisputed head of the household

Umsasane, umbrella thorn, flat crowned thorn tree, acacia

Umsululu, tree from which the gum is used in spear making

Umthakathi, witch, warlock, evil wizard, dark magic

Umzwilili; cape canary bird

Veld, type of wide open landscape in Southern Africa, a flat area covered in low grass and scrub

Yebo, yes

ACKNOWLEDGEMENTS

I would like to thank:

Patricia Lee Lewis, mentor and friend, for opening me to the possibility of a life as a writer. It has been her creative writing workshops held around the world, often in tandem with the wonderful Jacqueline Sheehan, that have provided the safe crucible in which this book was formed. I am also grateful to the participants in these workshops who showed courage and vulnerability in their own writing, which gave me permission to keep going deeper, (Patricia's website: www.writingretreats. org)

My friends who read the manuscript at various stages along the way and provided invaluable feedback, encouragement and support: Eva Dicassmiro, Viktoria Langton, Ian Macnaughton, Diana Gordon, Susan Wasserman, Michelle Fisk, and Shari Ulrich, who, at a critical moment late in the game, scraped me up off the floor when I was paralyzed with self-doubt and ready to throw the whole thing out,

My kindred friend, the profoundly talented Moira Walley-Beckett, for always believing in me,

Ian Macnaughton, healer and mentor, for being my lighthouse and guiding the way along the healing journey, for his kindness, compassion, big open heart, and for his deep understanding of the Tantric Path,

Carol Sill, for her knowledge of the self-publishing world and for shepherding me through the process with gentleness and good humour. Without her you would not be holding this book in your hands. And to my sister, Ann, who recommended I work with Carol,

Marsha Sidthorpe for caring and for helping with numerous submissions,

Diane G. Feught for the cover design of the book,

Jane Green for the back cover photograph,

Betsty Warland for accepting me into the Vancouver Manuscript Intensive program and for pairing me with Cathleen With, who was so generous with her patience and kindness and who understood my process.

About the Author

Jane Mortifee has been active as a singer and an actor in theatre, film, television and the studios doing voice-overs, jingles, and animated series. Nominated for an Actra Award, three Jessie Awards, a Westcoast Music Award, a Woman of Distinction Award, she has been inducted into the B.C. Entertainment Hall of Fame.

She has also performed in many solo concerts, as well as in various club bands over the years and has recorded three albums: *Conversations, Give Me Something Real,* and *Get Ready.*

Jane's focus now is leading yoga at various Creative Writing or Soul Collage retreats in Guatemala, Puerto Rico, New Zealand, Italy, Scotland and Mexico.

She is currently working on her second novel and her next album.

For more information please visit www.janemortifee.com.